THE GREAT COOKIE WAR

the GREAT COOKIE WAR

CAROLINE STELLINGS

Second Story Press

Library and Archives Canada Cataloguing in Publication

Title: The great cookie war / Caroline Stellings.
Names: Stellings, Caroline, 1961- author.
Identifiers: Canadiana (print) 20200332449 | Canadiana
   (ebook) 20200332457 | ISBN 9781772601732 (softcover) | ISBN
   9781772601749 (EPUB)
Classification: LCC PS8587.T4448 G74 2021 | DDC jC813/.6—dc23

Cover by Liz Parkes

Printed and bound in Canada

*Second Story Press gratefully acknowledges the support of the Ontario Arts
Council and the Canada Council for the Arts for our publishing program.
We acknowledge the financial support of the Government of Canada
through the Canada Book Fund.*

ONTARIO ARTS COUNCIL
CONSEIL DES ARTS DE L'ONTARIO

Canada Council   Conseil des Arts
for the Arts   du Canada

Funded by the Government of Canada
Financé par le gouvernement du Canada

Canada

MIX
Paper from
responsible sources
FSC   FSC® C103567

Published by
Second Story Press
20 Maud Street, Suite 401
Toronto, Ontario, Canada
M5V 2M5
www.secondstorypress.ca

For Dinah Hyrski and Kim Barnes,
two women I admire greatly

CHAPTER ONE

At night when darkness fell, and the winter winds swept across the open meadow, the wild things would come to the edge of the clearing. Mama left scraps for them; she said they were searching, always searching. At such an hour, our fieldstone house felt safe and warm—a refuge, an island of light and love in a cold sea of darkness. And yet, at such an hour, so many things crept into my mind, uninvited thoughts, thoughts I didn't want to have. Thoughts that arrived like the wild things, searching for something. I wondered what it would be like to live outside the Old Order, to not be a Mennonite. To use electric lights and ride in cars, not a horse-drawn buggy. To put on makeup, to have pierced ears. To go to the movies and out for pizza with other girls my age, and to be allowed to listen to music.

What I really wanted to do was paint. I wanted to become an artist. Sometimes I sketched, in my room, where no one could see me. I didn't have much to work with—just paper and pencils from school. But I drew everything I could see from my window: the row of sugar maples that grew beside our bank barn, the silver birches that lined the road to the silo, and sometimes just the clouds that floated slowly by. They observed me from above but never passed judgment. In summer, I would put crumbs on the ledge and try to sketch my blue jay friend before he took flight. Like the clouds, he didn't mind if I drew him. I think he liked it.

My parents and grandmother didn't understand the point in any of it. I am not sure if they thought it was sinful, but they felt that I should be doing something more important with my time. I knew that God could see me sketching, even if they could not, but it didn't feel like I was doing something wrong. At least, it didn't until I took that fall in the cutter. I shouldn't have tried driving it myself—I knew that—but I wanted to show my parents that I could do whatever my older brother could do.

They warned me, but I didn't listen. It wasn't Della's fault. She's a great horse. I pulled her into a tight turn, she stumbled, and over we went. I am glad she wasn't injured. And the doctor said my wrist would heal with time. I hoped so, prayed so, because it was my right hand that was hurt. My drawing hand. And one day— or so I hoped—my painting hand. Grand-mama never came out and said so, but I think she believed that it was God's way of expressing disapproval—not for taking the cutter, which could be excused as youth-ful folly, but for spending so much time sketching. Nothing could reduce my desire to become an artist, though. Nothing ever would. And even if my wrist always slowed me down, I would never let the pain stop me.

I suppose it was the same with all twelve-year-old girls, maybe we were all wondering, wanting, wishing. Maybe some girls wanted to scuba dive in the ocean or climb the Eiffel Tower. Maybe they wanted to go to Hollywood and become famous. Be someone other than who they were. Maybe we were all searching.

When morning came, and I saw the first rosy strips of light make their debut on the eastern horizon, those uninvited thoughts returned to the place they came from—the hardwood forest, or the orchard, or some such spot where they could hide from me during the day. They peeked out from behind a tree now and then, but didn't sit square on my shoulder as they did at night. The familiarity of morning drove them off, and reduced their strength. Thoughts that at night felt like great burning cravings for life outside the Order shrank down to chestnut-sized lumps of discontent during the day.

I took solace in that familiarity. It was a comfort that subdued my restlessness. I would wait to hear my mother's soft voice as she lifted my baby sister from her crib, and I would wait to smell kerosene in the lanterns as they were lit one by one, and bread baking, and coffee percolating in the big blue and white enamelware pot. I would wait for the stamping of snow from my father's boots as he carried in milk from the barn, and the crackle and bang of frozen logs being tossed into the wood stove by my brother. And the *yap*, *yap*, *yap* of Topper, our collie, barking out the window at the squirrels that had gathered around the base of the bird feeder.

"Beth! What are you doing up there? The breakfast table is waiting to be set."

And the sound of my grandmother, Grand-mama as we called her, making sure I didn't have too long to moon over my life. She didn't believe in daydreaming. "And young lady, could you fetch me some strawberry preserves from the cellar? Oh, and I'll be needing a few clean tea towels from the cupboard." When it came to chores, I was like the miller's daughter in Rumpelstiltskin—there was always more. If we Mennonites had framed family mottos on our walls they would all read the same: *If you have nothing to do, don't do it here.*

An island, a refuge. A place where nothing ever changed. Each morning, while I put on my black stockings and homespun dress, brushed and then braided my hair, I thought how Shakespeare was right when he wrote that the world is like a stage, and human beings are only actors. I felt like I was born into the Old Order, handed a script to memorize, and told by a director how to play my part. It wasn't that I didn't like that part, but I kept waiting for the play to end so that I could remove my costume and just be me.

And then I would ask myself again, *Why do you want your life to be different? Why do you want things to change?*

It was on a Saturday in February of 1984 when the choice was taken out of my hands, and my life finally did change. I remember that day like it was yesterday.

The morning began in the usual way, with my family rising early because it was market day, and we had to get our jams and jellies and pies and maple syrup and eggs and cheese and handiwork to St. Jacobs to sell to the droves of tourists that arrived weekly. While we lived a simple life, and asked for very little, sometimes it was hard for my parents to get by. My mother sewed everything we wore, and we grew most of our own food, but we still had to pay taxes. We still had to buy flour and sugar. My father still needed to pay for hardware and animal feed. And the more popular the St. Jacobs market became, the more vendors there were to choose from, which meant that my parents came home with less income each year.

The sky was a dull gray that day, when I pulled myself from under the quilt and reached for my warm underthings. Great winter squalls came bounding from the north and grabbed our house by the scruff of its neck, whipping it until the windows shook with dread. I was, in fact, grateful for the snow because whenever it rained, the ceiling over my bed leaked and the sound of the dripping kept me awake at night. My father would be putting on a new roof with the help of local men, but first he needed to buy the shingles.

They were expensive, and something he couldn't manufacture himself.

As I dressed, Mama and Papa were already loading up our wares into crates; soon they'd be riding with me in the back of our big sleigh, hitched to Della. I thought about how my mother dreaded having to go to the market. She would never say so, and I never did ask her what she thought, but for my parents, despite having to endure the stares of tourists who weren't used to our old-fashioned style of dressing, the market was their only chance to sell the goods we grew or baked or created. For me, spending Saturday at the market wasn't only a way to visit the outside world—it was a trip to my own personal paradise.

Once, I saw a girl with a beautiful paint box. The kind that professionals use. She must have purchased it from one of the vendors because the price tag of thirty-five dollars was still on the pan of watercolors. It appeared to contain a dozen or more squares of brilliant colors, and they were from a company called Winsor and Newton. She had a block of high-quality paper and fabulous brushes, too, all peeking out of her canvas shopping bag. Oh, how I envied that girl. I knew that jealousy was not a good thing, but the emotion came over me with great intensity and swept me away like a sandcastle in a tidal wave.

Ordinarily my whole family went to the market to-gether—my older brother Isaiah, younger sister Sarah, and even the baby Rebecca—but on this Saturday, my grandmother thought better of it.

"Leave her here with me, Livvy," she told my moth-er. "The cold will catch the both of us. Then I'll be gone. Pushing up daisies." Grand-mama often threat-ened us with her demise, but she was as strong as Della, and enjoyed a similar constitution. Slender as she was, and always complaining that nothing set well with her, she could eat more than any of us and was never sick a day in her life.

A branch from our huge oak tree broke off and crashed against the house. I shuddered, and Isaiah ran to look out the window. My parents carried on as usual; they didn't let winter weather trouble them too much. And my grandmother positively thrived on it.

"I tell you, that storm is going to be as bad as we've ever seen. And this winter, we've seen it all."

"What makes you say that, Mother?" asked my father.

"I know by the way the wind feels and by the color of the eastern sky." Grand-mama shook her head in a menacing sort of way, but I could tell she was looking forward to it. "The youngest and I will stay here today."

"I'd rather have the baby with me," protested Mama.

"They keep that building too warm, and not for the locals," said Grand-mama. "I remember the days when they held the market out of doors. All year round. Now, the tourists demand July temperatures in the middle of winter, then climb back into their heated automobiles. I say it's too much of a shock to bring an infant out of a heated arena into the bitter cold."

"You know she won't be reckoned with," said my father, looking at Mama from over his glasses. "Isaiah, you stay here with your grandmother and the baby. I don't like the idea of leaving them here alone in case that storm arrives sooner than expected."

"I'll be fine," said Grand-mama. "It's cold all right, but I can deal with the snow. It won't turn to ice rain for a few days." She looked out the window. "I can tell by that haze in the east."

"Isaiah," said my father, "I'd like you to clean the barn today. It has to be done, and that way you can be here with your grandmother and Rebecca."

"I will make *knepp*, and maybe another *schnitz* pie while you are gone," Grand-mama said, turning her attention to the porridge that was bubbling and squeaking on the range. "I used up the end of the oats, Livvy," she told my mother. "A little more water than usual, and there's enough here to feed us all." I think most members of my community try not to be wasteful, especially the older ladies, like my grandmother, who lived during hard times. She once told us that in her day, a woman was allowed one yeast cake when she got married and had to keep it going until the day she died. I didn't think it possible, but she swore that the starter she used in her bread could trace its ancestry to a fermented concoction from fifty years before.

Although she often watered down the cereal, and claimed to be the most frugal woman in Waterloo County, I knew that her potato dumplings were light because she used more eggs than the recipe called for, and I once saw her dump a full cup of heavy cream into her apple pie filling when my mother wasn't watching. Of course, things like butter, cream, and eggs were plentiful for us, because we were farmers. I don't believe I ever saw her use more than a thimble-full of vanilla extract—that we had to pay for. And although Mennonites are not supposed to boast, she took pride in her baking and was known throughout the region for it, thanks to an author by the name of Edna Staebler. A good friend to my family, she visited us often and wrote a cookbook about what we ate and how we prepared it. It was called *Food That Really Schmecks*—which means food that tastes great. It sold a million copies!

Isaiah walked across the long kitchen to the cookstove, at which my grandmother was working. "Will you make *fetschpatze*?" My brother loved donuts, especially dunked in maple syrup. But then, my brother loved food in general.

"I will leave two pies here for us," said my mother. "I have more than enough to sell."

"Never enough," said my father, taking his place at the head of the table.

My younger sister reached for the apple butter and began putting globs of it onto her plate.

"Sarah!" my mother scolded. "You won't eat all that." She took the serving dish from her. Wasting food is not allowed in our home. In any Mennonite home for that matter. "And we haven't said grace."

Once the clatter of action at the stove stopped, and we were seated at the long pine table, we bowed our heads in a silent prayer. The only sound came from the baby, who chortled and gurgled the whole time, and Topper, lapping up his morning bowl of milk. I was thankful for my family and for the food. I was thankful that it was market day, and I could meet people from outside our community. I tried not to hope for anything other than what I had. I tried not to hope for my life to change.

Everyone reached for a piece of bread except Sarah who ate the apple butter by itself, then oatmeal with butter on top. My mother gazed first at her, then Grand-mama, and then the baby. She did not want to leave Rebecca at home, but she knew that my grandmother would have the last word.

"I'd like to sell two or three dozen gallons of syrup," said my father. "In another month or so, we'll be gathering the new crop. Hard to believe a whole year has gone by since we last fired up the sugar shack."

"I think syrup tastes better the older it gets," said Grand-mama. According to her, the only things that didn't improve with age were ice cream and dirty socks. "Don't be giving it away at a discount, David. I never have enough for my baking, never enough."

"Why do the tourists like the early sap?" my brother asked.

"It tastes more like the tree," offered Sarah, and my parents smiled.

Mama wiped some gruel from the baby's chin,

then looked at me. "You're not eating much these days, Beth. Are you feeling all right?"

"She's been spending too much time upstairs in her room," said Grand-mama. "Dreaming up pictures, of all things."

"I am not dreaming up things," I said. "I paint what I see."

"Don't talk back to your grandmother," said Papa.

"Last night you barely touched your food, child. You have no appetite. I will bake a cinnamon coffee cake for when you come back from St. Jacobs." Grand-mama dumped a large glob of oatmeal into my bowl, then poured cream over it. "You are far too thin."

"What is wrong with paintings?" I asked. "Why must the walls be bare?"

"Modesty is the most important virtue a person can have," said my father.

I thought about his comment for a moment, then asked, "We have colorful quilts. I have seen some that are very decorative. What is the difference?"

As soon as I asked the question, I felt embarrassed for my father because he seemed to have no answer.

Grand-mama replied for him. "Quilts are useful. We cannot live without them." She poured more cream on my cereal. "I think your artistic inclinations could be put to good use if you were to spend more time on needlework and less time drawing things for no reason."

There was no way to make her see my point of view, so I said nothing and ate as much breakfast as I was able, then put my bowl down for Topper to finish off. By the way my parents were looking at me, I could tell they were thinking it was my age, something I would outgrow. My mother probably went through it herself. Maybe even Grand-mama, although that was a long time ago, and I think my people didn't know very much about the outside world back then.

When it came right down to it, I didn't know much about the outside world myself. How could I? I went to a Mennonite school, attended a Mennonite church, and all my friends were Mennonites. Other than the tourists at the market—and they had ten times as many questions about us than we did about them—I only enjoyed one connection to life outside Waterloo County, and that was Edna Staebler. She lived a couple of miles down the road from us, in a cozy little cottage on Sunfish Lake.

And it was Edna who, on that Saturday in February, brought a woman to the market with her to meet my family. She looked to be thirty years old and her hair was styled like I'd never seen before in real life, only on the front of magazines that were sold in the market and in the general store. This woman had on a bright yellow suit and fancy shoes to match. Even the wealthiest of tourists with whom I had done business didn't have clothes like that. And along with a purse, she carried a briefcase.

I spotted Edna and the woman long before they reached our stall, and wondered who the stranger could be. I thought she might be another writer, or maybe someone from the office of the company that published Edna's books. She moved briskly, nervously, almost as if fleeing down a track from an oncoming train. She was even faster than Edna, who, despite being nearly eighty years of age, was well-known for the spring in her step.

This woman didn't waste any time in getting right to the point.

"Hello," she offered, flicking a speck of lint from her skirt. She looked, and even smelled, urban; her perfume reminded me of violets I collected in the meadow, only two thousand times as intense. Before Edna had a chance to introduce her, she did it herself. "I am Paula Logan, and I need to talk to you about cookies."

Cookies? No one could be in that much of a rush for cookies. And we didn't even bring cookies to market. The tourists wanted pies, cheese, maple syrup, needlework—but not cookies.

"Cookies?" replied my mother. "We have no—"

"Cookies. I want to talk to you about your cookies." The woman looked at me. I shrugged, then smiled.

Edna brushed past a group of women. They were holding out one of our full-sized quilts, turning it over and over again, examining the stitching so carefully you'd think they were checking for fleas. On the one hand, they couldn't stop gawking at my mother's odd-to-them dress and stockings, but on the other, they couldn't get over the sophistication of the work that had gone into that quilt.

"David, Livvy…." There was an apologetic tone to our friend's voice. "This is Paula—"

"Logan," interrupted the woman. Her amber eyes flashed. "I am an attorney with the firm of Knowles, Roseburg, Johnson, and Kenyon." She stuck out her hand. "I need to speak to you." Her head bounced from side to side. "In private."

In private? The building was packed already, and hundreds more clambered to get through the doors. Other than a washroom stall, there was nowhere anyone could carry on a confidential conversation. I thought hard but couldn't figure out how the topic of cookies might involve classified information.

My parents stood stock-still. It took nearly a solid minute for my father to extend his hand. He wasn't being rude, it just took that long to process her remark.

My little sister held out her hand, too. She didn't know it was just for adults.

"Miss Logan would like to ask you a few questions," offered Edna. "And yes, it does involve your cookies."

CHAPTER TWO

"**C**ookies are big business," explained the lawyer. "And *Mother's Best* is one of the most popular brands in North America."

Cookies. I was disappointed that her eagerness to talk to us was about stupid old cookies. I had been imagining that she owned an art gallery in Toronto or Montreal, and was scouting around for new talent.

We watched as she took out a roll of tablets from her purse and tossed two of them into her mouth. "Antacids. I live on them." She looked at my mother. "You must have them in your cupboard?"

"Antacids?" Mama was puzzled. Other than the occasional stomach upset when we ate too many of Grand-mama's walnut squares (she used a quarter-pound of butter in every batch), members of my family were not prone to indigestion.

"Cookies. *Mother's Best* cookies." She pulled away from my sister, who'd been inspecting the hem of her skirt, turning it over like the women had done with the quilt. Mama grabbed Sarah's hand when she realized what was happening. We Mennonites are known for being well-behaved. Edna once told Grand-mama how impressed she was by our disposition. She said that so many of her friends' grandchildren were restless all of the time, constantly in motion, swinging on the back of their mother's chair and whining until it drove everyone in the room completely mad. Not us!

"We bake cookies," I replied politely. "We don't buy them."

"Right, yeah," said the lawyer.

Edna spoke up. "That's why Miss Logan is here," she said. "All the way from Manhattan."

That was the moment of Miss Paula Logan's coronation, for in my mind, she instantly became royalty. I had met tourists from Toronto, Buffalo, Niagara Falls, and Rochester. But never New York.

Some of the best galleries in the world are in New York City.

"Have you ever been to the Metropolitan Museum of Art?" I forgot myself momentarily, and by the look on my mother's face, I knew I had spoken out of turn. "I mean, Miss Logan, have you ever—?"

"Call me Paula."

I looked at my father. We were not encouraged to call adults by their first name, and yet we were also supposed to do what they told us to do. This left me in a bit of a conundrum, which was complicated by the fact that neither of my parents answered my question. Since I was used to addressing Edna by her first name, I figured on doing the same with the lady lawyer. I waited for my parents' approval, but they were still trying to figure out what this woman wanted from them, and where cookies entered into the picture.

"May I?" I asked. My father shrugged, which I took as a "yes," since if it had been a "no" he would have been more definite about it.

"And yes," she said. "I've been to the museum many times. It's on the eastern edge of Central Park, not far from where I work."

"Whose paintings have you seen there?" I asked.

"Picasso, Matisse, Monet—so many," she replied. "Not only at the Met, but also the Museum of Modern Art, the Guggenheim, and other galleries."

Picasso. Matisse. Monet. The greatest artists that ever lived.

And she has seen their paintings in person. Up close.

Paula Logan's world was so different from mine. It was just as if she was beckoning me to a new land, inviting me to discover its many treasures.

She might as well have been the Statue of Liberty.

"I read that the Metropolitan Museum has two million paintings in its collection." My parents looked surprised that I knew so much about art.

"Do you paint?" asked the lawyer.

"I sketch." I glanced at my father. "Here and there."

"Good for you," she said.

Suddenly, I had a terrific feeling of godly accomplishment.

She pulled a file from her briefcase, then rested it on our stand between bottles of raspberry jam and two apple crumb pies. My mother moved the pies to a table behind her, since we always left them uncovered until sold, at which time we boxed them. She was probably afraid they'd be knocked off, and we couldn't afford to lose them. As for me, I wanted to ask Paula Logan a million questions about art but could tell she was in a big hurry to discuss cookies, or rather, the business of cookies. "So these *rigglevake*...

is that how you say it? Rig-gel-vake? And it means railroad?" She looked from side to side. "I really wish we could talk about this privately. I might have been followed."

Followed? Really? Over rigglevake cookies?

Edna spoke up. "I don't think it was a good idea to come here." She was beginning to question her judgment about bringing this lawyer to see us. Ever since her cookbook had become famous, she was quite protective of us—of all her Mennonite friends—because she unintentionally created a sort of public fascination about our way of life. People were starting to line up at our stall, and Edna realized we needed to attend to them or they would move on to another vendor. We didn't have time to be standing around. "David, Livvy," she said, "please carry on with your work. We will meet up with you at another time."

"Another time?" What for us was the mad confusion of the St. Jacobs market, must for this woman from Manhattan have seemed like a good place to meditate. "I have to be back in the office early next week." Paula looked from side to side again, this time scrutinizing every man, woman, and child within earshot. I didn't know at that point that my family and I would soon be drawn into the world of corporate espionage, but my life was suddenly becoming much more interesting than it had ever been.

She waited for my parents to deal with the customers in line, and became impatient when one woman haggled with them over the price of a shoofly pie. This woman claimed that there wasn't enough molasses in it because it wasn't as dark as others she had seen in the marketplace. My mother attempted to explain that the apple molasses we use is lighter in color than ordinary blackstrap and actually makes for a better pie.

Paula took a notepad from her purse and started jotting things down. I heard her mumble something about having a sample of apple molasses sent for analysis to a lab in New Jersey.

"Well, I don't know," said the woman. "I have eaten many shoofly pies in my day, but I never—"

"I can believe it," Paula said, loud enough that the woman heard her and walked away in an obvious huff.

"Oh, no," said Edna. "Now you've lost a sale."

"Yes." My father put the pie back in its crate, and began moving cans of maple syrup to the front of our stall. My mother helped him.

"I will reimburse you," said the lawyer. "In fact, I have a contract here that assures that you will be well paid for your time and any out-of-pocket expenses you might incur."

I noticed my father and mother exchange glances when the woman said they'd be paid for their time.

"Contract?" I turned to Edna, and she rested her hand on my shoulder.

"Providing your parents agree to it," she told me. Then she spoke directly to my mother. "You don't need to sign anything, Liv. Just a verbal agreement will suffice."

"For now." Paula moved her briefcase to the ground between her feet. She handed Edna her purse, then began rifling through another file, this one thicker than the first. I found it hard to believe that there could be so much paperwork around something as everyday as cookies. The lawyer kept looking over her shoulder, but I think by then she'd realized that she had better say what she'd come to say, or risk never getting the chance. The look on Edna's face told me that she was just about to put an end to the whole thing.

"The lawsuit rests upon a patent." The lawyer gestured with her pen. "A patent for doughs and cookies providing storage-stable texture variability."

Lawsuit?

Storage-stable texture variability?

"*Mother's Best*," explained Edna, "is being sued by another multinational company, *Baker's Pride*."

My sister, tired of the conversation, was fast becoming one of those kids that swung on a chair and whined. She held on to my father's leg, looked up at him, and yawned.

I wasn't bored in the least.

"We're talking millions of dollars at stake," said the lawyer. She said it in a matter-of-fact way, but her expression changed when a man and woman, who'd been trying to decide which size of maple syrup was the best price per fluid ounce, overheard her remark.

"Wow," joked the man, "that'll buy a lot of sap."

Paula snapped the file shut and stuffed it into her briefcase.

After the couple had paid for their syrup and walked away, the lawyer made plans to meet with us at our home. My parents were reluctant at first, but there seemed to be no way around it. No way around Paula Logan, either.

"This is in the hands of the courts, and you could be subpoenaed," she advised my parents.

Subpoenaed?

Edna didn't take kindly to the threat.

"My Mennonite friends do not go to court," she

declared. "And when I agreed to introduce you to them, I made it clear that it was only for information about the cookies." I don't think Paula understood that other than church, wakes, and childbirth, Mennonites tried to avoid definite appointments.

"Do you want us to bake them for you?" I asked.

Edna nodded. "That's part of it."

"A small part," declared Paula, which led me to believe that anything we knew so far was only the tip of what would prove to be one massive and convoluted iceberg. "I will see you tomorrow," she said.

"Not tomorrow." My mother spoke quietly. "We don't do business on the Sabbath."

"We aren't doing business," replied the lawyer acidly. "Not yet, anyway."

"It involves business," said my father. "We will see you Monday afternoon."

"Not until Monday afternoon?" Paula rolled her eyes.

"I'm sorry, Miss, but I have my chores. And there's a raising out near Floradale. We have to get a start on it. Even the bad weather won't stop it from going forward."

"Right," said Edna. "The Martins lost their barn to a fire, and the men will be rebuilding it as fast as they can. They have livestock that are surviving in temporary shelter until that can be done."

"Why can't they get a contractor to build it?"

"My Mennonite friends don't carry commercial insurance. They look out for each other."

Paula wrinkled her forehead in a befuddled sort of way. "So the men will build this barn on Monday?"

"We'll get the beams in place," said my father. "Then we'll mill the boards soon after that."

"And Livvy will be helping to feed them all," said Edna. "Am I right?"

"You are," replied Mama. "We're starting early in the morning. We'll be back around three or four."

"What will I do until then?" Paula rolled her eyes again.

Edna smiled. "I will show you around the area. Maybe you'd like to see the covered bridge in West Montrose. It's the oldest one in Canada. And quite long."

"Not as long as this weekend is going to be." She picked up her briefcase, and took her purse from Edna's arm. Then she clicked it open, found the roll of antacids, and threw two of them into her mouth. "I guess I have no choice." She pointed at my mother's head. "You have to wear that hat all the time?" She then pivoted to face Edna. "What is that thing called?"

"Mennonite ladies wear organdie caps because, in the Bible, St. Paul says that women must keep their heads covered while praying," she explained.

Paula looked baffled. I knew she was trying to figure out why such a cap had to be worn every day of the week, and all day long. Realizing that what she needed was a codebreaker, I decided to offer an explanation.

"We pray a lot," I said.

CHAPTER THREE

The moment we arrived home, I jumped from the sleigh and raced into the kitchen to tell my brother what happened at the market. The sun had already sunk beneath the western horizon, and the windows of our kitchen were glowing from the light of the kerosene lanterns that blazed within. Isaiah was stacking small logs beside the wood stove at which my grandmother was busy stirring a pot of carrot soup; the baby was seated in her highchair at the table, bashing a spoon against the side of her bowl.

"You'll never guess what happened!" I kicked off my boots, and snow flew in every direction. Topper ate lumps of it like it was ice cream. My brother laughed as he took a cloth from his overalls to wipe his hands.

"You get a broom and clean that up now," scolded Grand-mama. "I don't want to take a fall. That's about all I need at my age." She took a small sip from the soup ladle, then reached for a sprig of dried dill weed that hung from a nail near the pantry. "That'll be right," she said, tossing it into the pot.

"Are neither one of you curious about my news?" I pulled a broom from the closet, but rather than sweeping with it, I felt like clobbering my brother.

Clutching a half-eaten banana and as relaxed as a cat, Isaiah sat himself down at the table, leaned back in his chair, and with a slight yawn, asked, "So what's the big deal?" He inherited my parents' genes for calmness, every one of them, and left none for me.

"This woman, Edna brought her. She's a lawyer, all the way from New York City. She's coming here on Monday to learn about our railroad cookies. She's going to pay us to bake them!" I swept the snow into a dustpan, then tossed it outside. The wind made a whooshing sound as I opened the door. "It's really important, too. She had files and everything." I put my hands on my knees to catch a breath.

My parents and sister brushed by me on their way in, and Mama headed straight for Rebecca. She picked her up and gave her a big hug. The baby gurgled and kicked her feet, and Mama kissed her cheek. Topper let out a loud bark when he saw Papa was home.

"You hopped out of the sleigh so fast, Beth, that you left your new scarf behind," my father said, rubbing Topper's back heartily. Mama had knitted it for me as a Christmas present; it was pink and white, and while I liked it very much, everything I had was homemade. I knew that I should have been grateful because there are people in the world who don't have such things, but there was a part of me that wanted to own store-bought clothes.

Papa hung my scarf on the coatrack, then peered into the soup pot to see what was boiling. "I suppose Beth has told you all about the woman we met today," he said. Then he removed Sarah's jacket, and sat her on a stool so that he could pull off her boots.

Grand-mama ignored my father's comment, and in an I-don't-care-to-hear-about-a-woman-from-New-York sort of way, turned the subject around to weather. "I hope everything sold today. With the storm that's coming, there may be no one at the market next weekend. Did you see the size of that ring around the moon?" We did not have a radio, but Grand-mama always managed to give us an accurate forecast. Nature told her all she needed to know, and she'd been warning us since November that we were in for a doozy of a winter. She knew because the squirrels had fluffier tails than she'd ever seen, and the pine trees had formed twice as many cones as usual. At that moment, however, I couldn't have cared less about weather.

"This is the most exciting thing that has ever happened," I said. "Her name is Paula Logan and her client is a big company called *Mother's Best*."

"I've seen those cookies." Isaiah spoke like a man of the world. "I saw them on television."

"Television?" asked my mother.

"Every time I help the men deliver their chairs to the furniture shop in Kitchener, I stop to look at those things. They have rows and rows of them, and they all go at once."

"All that noise and clatter—reminds me of this lady lawyer," mumbled my father.

"I hope I'm back from school in time to meet her," said Isaiah. And then, showing more emotion than I'd seen since the time he was able to axe through a fourteen-inch stump single-handedly, he added, "I don't believe I've ever met someone like that."

"Me neither," said Sarah, but I don't think she really knew why.

"No school for you on Monday, son," said my father. "We'll be needing you to help with the barn raising."

"Mama and Papa will be at the Martins' all day on Monday," I said, "so Edna won't be bringing her here until later in the day. Isn't that great?" I paused. "That way I can find out what's going on."

My grandmother shook her head. "You concentrate on your schoolwork, you hear? Not some crazy notion about cookies." She frowned. "And don't be so happy about a barn raising. This is a difficult time for the Martins."

My brother nodded in agreement. "Still, I hope she brings us a few boxes of those *Mother's Best* cookies to try!"

Food. All my brother ever thinks about is food.

"What do you want with those fool things?" Grandmama made it clear that she wasn't keen on the idea of a big-city lawyer coming to call, and she certainly didn't approve of store-bought cookies. "And what on earth does this woman want from us?"

"I don't know, exactly," replied my father. "Apparently, it's about the family recipe for rigglevake cookies."

"She came all the way from New York City to talk about rigglevake cookies? There's something mighty peculiar about that." Grand-mama retrieved her little black book from the drawer in which she kept it, not far from her baking table. It was a family treasure that had traveled all the way from Pennsylvania in 1850 with her great-great-grandmother, and was so old that many of its yellowed pages were just hanging by a thread. My grandmother knew all the recipes by heart—my mother did as well—so they didn't rely on the book very much. Once in a while, they would look through it to refresh their memories, or to recall a pie or cake they might have forgotten about. The book, though, was mostly symbolic. It stood as a constant and concrete reminder of our heritage.

The only person outside our family ever to lay hands on that book was Edna Staebler. The respect she had for our culture ran deep, and when she wrote about us in magazines it was not to entertain the public, but rather to present our life in such a way that others could understand and appreciate us. She wrote about why we didn't believe in war, and why we preferred to live simply, and why we thrived on hard work. Grand-mama trusted Edna Staebler—they had been good friends for a long time—so she had allowed the author to copy out the recipes for her cookbook.

Grand-mama searched through until she found

the cookie section and read the one for rigglevakes out loud. "Light part…flour, sugar, eggs, butter, vanilla." She shrugged her shoulders. "Dark part…molasses… yes, yes…." She read it over to herself, then set the book down on the cupboard. "You roll them up, cut and bake them, and they look like wheels." She turned to my mother. "So what?"

"She wants to know how to bake them," I said.

"Grand-mama can teach her how to do that," said Isaiah.

"No one comes all that way to learn how to bake cookies." My grandmother was suspicious of outsiders anyway, so Paula Logan had a mark against her before she even set foot in the door. Neither my father nor my mother dared to mention the lawsuit, and the term "storage-stable texture variability" never crossed their lips. And while my mind was bounding between cookies and the Guggenheim Museum—even the name was exciting—I think my parents were praying that they hadn't done the wrong thing in allowing the lawyer to visit us on Monday.

If Paula Logan thought her weekend would go on forever, it was nothing like the one I experienced. The minutes crept by. I was always a little bit restless during the morning service at our Meetinghouse anyway, but on that Sunday, it was like watching grass grow. I always tried to keep my mind on what the preacher was telling us about immorality, but somehow managed to come out feeling like a worse sinner than I was before going in, because I could never remember what he said. Not all of it, anyway.

For the most part, the message was always the same: to be humble and work hard and not expect too much out of life. I had the first two directives down pat. I worked around the farm—I helped with cooking, canning, and cleaning, and I tended the garden in summer—and I would say I kept fairly humble. But not expecting too much out of life was where I fell down on the job of being a Mennonite. I didn't for the first ten years of my life, but once my friend Elizabeth Eby brought a big photographic book to school, and I learned about the history of art, it all changed. She lent the book to me once, for a whole weekend, and although Grand-mama wasn't pleased, I read it from cover to cover at least two dozen times. I learned more about art that weekend than most people do in a lifetime.

So when Paula Logan said she had actually stood in front of some of the most famous paintings in the world, it was no wonder that Monday couldn't come soon enough for me. As it was, I had another long wait in class all day before I could find out what was happening.

Sarah and I were lucky to get a ride home in Ann Weber's cutter—that speeded things up nicely. Ann's grandfather had been out to the barn raising at the Martin farm and passed the schoolhouse on his way back from Floradale.

"We've got the beams in place," he hollered back from the driver's seat. "Once we get a break in the weather, we'll have it up in a jiffy." He jostled the reins to keep his horse moving over a patch of ice. "They poured the foundation just in the nick of time, I'd say."

"Have you ever driven this cutter?" I asked Ann.

"I did try once," she said. "With my father next to me."

"What happened?" I asked.

"Well," she replied with a smile, "it was a good thing I wasn't on the road."

"You can say that again," hollered her grandfather. "We lost three of our newly planted saplings."

"I won't be driving a cutter again," I said. "Not after

what happened to me." I watched as Ann's grandfather deftly maneuvered his horse to the left to avoid a snowbank. "I steered sharply and we overturned."

"Your Della is a gentle horse, though," added Ann, and I nodded in agreement.

"Oh, she's great. She's never given my father any trouble at all." I shrugged. "It was my fault," I admitted. "I don't think she'd be too happy to see me taking the reins again."

"I want to ride Della," said Sarah. "I could do it, you just watch me."

"Don't you girls rush your life away," shouted Ann's grandfather. "The future will be here soon enough."

He stopped at the end of our lane and we jumped out. From the road, I spotted Edna's car, which meant that she and Paula Logan had arrived. I did not see any tracks in the snow from our buggy, just those made by the automobile.

"Mr. Weber," I asked, "were my parents and brother still at the Martin farm when you left?"

"They were indeed," he said, looking back at Ann to be sure she was securely in place. "Your mama was just finishing up with the ladies. They should be back from Floradale shortly." He gave the horse a firm tap, and off they went.

"Thanks!" I called. Then I grabbed Sarah by the arm and began to scurry down the lane.

"I can't run that fast!" she complained.

She dropped one of her books and stopped to pick it up.

"Come on!"

"What's wrong?" she said.

"The lady lawyer and Edna are alone. No one is there to help them."

"Grand-mama is there," said Sarah.

"That's what I mean! We've got to hurry!"

CHAPTER FOUR

"That's what happens when you don't pay your hydro bill," kidded Paula. "Just tell them your check must have been lost in the mail." There was a pause. "You do use the mail service, don't you? Don't tell me you rely on the Pony Express!"

Those were the first words I heard when I came through the door. My grandmother looked like she had drunk a glass of lemonade in which she'd skimped on sugar. Edna looked like she'd sent someone a condolence card by mistake for their birthday. The lawyer was the only one smiling—at least she was, until she realized that no one was laughing at her joke.

"Well, I mean, there's no electricity! Not even so much as a forty-watt bulb!"

"That's right," said Grand-mama, "and we like it that way." Her eyes blazed, but her voice was as unemotional as a scrambled egg. Thankfully, the kettle whistled her back to the stove to prepare tea. One thing about us Mennonites, we feed any and all visitors, even if we don't like them too much.

"Can you tell the time of day from where shadows fall?" asked Paula. That wasn't a joke. I think she assumed we used sundials. In her defense, I would say that ironstone plates, pictureless walls, and an oilcloth-covered table would lead anyone to believe they'd just stepped out of a time machine and found themselves back about a hundred years.

"How was school today?" Edna asked me. It was obvious she was trying to change the subject.

"Not bad," I replied, although frankly, I couldn't remember a single moment of that exceptionally long day. I wondered if the weekend had been long for the lawyer, too. After what she'd said at the market, it must have felt like a year.

"Did you make it to the covered bridge at West Montrose?" I asked.

"No," said Edna, "I had some unexpected visitors, and with the weather being the way it is, they wound up staying overnight." She turned to Paula. "I do want you to see it before you leave. It's a sight to behold."

"I'd like to come also," I said. I had been over the bridge hundreds of times, but never with someone from New York City. And I figured it might be a golden opportunity to have a chance to talk with her alone, away from Grand-mama, and ask her a lot of questions about art. "It's not too far from here. Maybe we could take you in the sleigh. Or the cutter. I get home from school by mid-afternoon. I could ask my father if he'd take us."

"Your father can't be driving around on a weekday afternoon," said my grandmother in a sullen sort of way. She was still angry over the hydro remark.

"Maybe Isaiah could drive us?"

"No, Beth. Your brother has his chores."

"I can't drive the cutter," I said apologetically.

"I should say not," said Grand-mama. "You nearly got yourself killed the last time you tried, and that was right in our own laneway! I can't bear to think what might have happened had you been on the road."

"Don't you need a license?" asked Paula, in a voice that indicated she was only marginally interested in my reply.

"No," I said with a glance at my grandmother. "Not to drive a horse."

"And wagon?" Paula asked. I fully expected her next question to be whether instead of gas stations, we had places to fill up our horses with hay.

"I think you mean a buggy," I said. "Or a cutter in winter. We don't really drive wagons, at least not since our ancestors came here from Pennsylvania." Edna gave a little laugh, and I suppose it sounded funny, but I was really just telling it like it was.

"In this kind of weather," said my grandmother, "no one should be out in the cutter. Not even an experienced driver. It wouldn't take much for an accident to happen. If some crazy motorist was to slide into Della...." She shook a finger at me. "Then we'd all be in trouble, wouldn't we? How'd we get to church?" Grand-mama opened the oven door, tapped lightly on one of the buns to see if it sounded hollow (which meant they were done), and lifted the pan to a cooling rack.

"Boy, do they smell good," said Edna. "With your parents' permission, you can come along with us to the bridge tomorrow. Paula is going to attempt to make the cookies, too, so it would be nice to have your help with that. You can tell us where we're going wrong." She gave me a little wink. "We'll wait until you are back from school." She turned to Grand-mama. "We'll take my car to the bridge."

Paula didn't seem too concerned as to whether she made it to West Montrose or not, and cared even less if I came along. She was only interested in the lawsuit. I figured that before anyone had a chance to carry the conversation back to rigglevake cookies, I'd better put in my bid to talk about art instead.

"Have you ever seen a painting by Vincent van Gogh?" I asked quickly. From what I had read in Elizabeth Eby's book, he was considered by some experts to be the best artist of all time.

"I did. I saw *Starry Night* at the Museum of Modern Art. It was glorious."

Glorious. I decided that I would remember that word. I wanted to paint something that was glorious one day.

"Speaking of art," said Edna, "we have a very fine artist here in Waterloo. His name is Peter Etril Snyder and he is quite good."

"He's a Mennonite." I looked at Grand-mama when I said that, but she didn't bat an eye. She carried the teapot to the table and began dusting her cinnamon rolls with powdered sugar.

"I've never heard of him," said Paula.

"He studied at the Ontario College of Art in Toronto," Edna remarked.

I had no hope of attending a school like that. It was totally out of reach for me.

"Beth is a girl," said Grand-mama. I didn't need reminding.

Edna was always courteous about our ways, but was equally respectful of women's rights. She believed that girls should never be kept from pursuing their dreams. I figured she'd find a way to politely counter my grandmother's comment, and she did.

"I know of a Mennonite woman artist—Agatha Loewen Duerksen Schmidt is her name," she said. "She is known especially for her painting *Exodus*. It is a beautiful piece that depicts her experience as a refugee, fleeing from the Soviet Union."

"I would love to meet her," I said, "and maybe I will meet Peter Etril Snyder one day too."

"We'll have to visit his gallery sometime." Edna smiled at me. "With your parents' permission, of course." She thought for a moment. "I heard that he began painting when he was twelve years old."

Before I could respond, Grand-mama expressed her disapproval. "What on earth is the point of it all?" she argued.

Neither Edna nor I had a fast answer. I knew that art was important but couldn't explain why.

Paula, however, had no problem coming up with a reply. Being a natural-born debater, she couldn't help but argue the point.

"You must ask yourself why so many of the Old Masters painted landscapes, portraits, and so on," she said. "I believe it is because the emotional response is what matters. Words are not the only way to touch the human soul. A person must visualize something to truly understand it."

I waited for my grandmother to yell "Objection," and Paula to return with "Overruled!"

Edna and I glanced at each other, but neither one of us said anything. It was Paula who broke the silence.

"Well, they say a picture is worth a thousand words." She shrugged.

Grand-mama didn't agree with any of it. "We prefer to keep things simple here," was all she said. Then she placed a large platter of rolls in the middle of the table.

"You baked those without electricity?" Paula asked, pulling out a chair and pointing to the buns. She sat down and took her notepad out of her purse, along with a pen, and placed it beside her napkin. I guessed that she would be taking notes as to how we baked in general, not just cookies. Edna sat beside her, and I seated myself across from the both of them.

"My Grand-mama can bake anything in the world," said Sarah. She stuck her hand in the cookie jar, yanked out two oatmeal raisin squares, squeezed them together to make one, and then clunked down next to me.

"All I know for sure is that I'd love to learn to paint," I said. I glanced at my grandmother to get her reaction. There wasn't one. She was either still fuming over the hydro issue or trying to think of a comeback to our discussion about Agatha Loewen Duerksen Schmidt.

"Mrs. Gladstone in Elmira takes students," offered Edna. "She's been teaching art lessons for fifty years. Some of her students are good enough to enter their work into the county fair competition."

Paula made a face. I don't think old Mrs. Gladstone impressed her too much.

My grandmother made a worse face.

"Young girls have more important things to learn." Grand-mama made art sound like something shameful, like athlete's foot. "Surely you must have learned your lesson by now—" She wanted to say something about my wrist being injured, that I should not be using my hand for frivolous activities, but she stopped short.

After checking to be sure the table was fully set, my grandmother pulled the square out of Sarah's mouth, returned it to her plate, and then sat down for grace.

Paula looked from side to side; she probably didn't know we gave thanks silently. Edna knew, and must have kicked Paula under the table because after a slight knee jerk, Paula dropped her head.

Once my grandmother raised her head, Paula tasted a bun. "This cinnamon roll is so light, I practically have to hold it down to take a bite." She took a swig of tea, swallowed quickly, and took another huge bite. "I hope these don't cause heartburn."

"Heartburn!" I thought Grand-mama was going to stab the lawyer with her butter knife.

"They are delicious," said Edna. Deftly dodging the heartburn remark, she steered the talk back to art. "I've known you for all these years, Beth, and didn't realize that you wanted to be an artist," she said.

"Oh, yes. I would give anything to be able to take those lessons," I said. I turned to Grand-mama. "I would be sure they didn't interfere with my chores. Or take time away from learning other things."

"Classes like that would be expensive," said Grand-mama. "We can't be spending money on something like that." I knew it wasn't just the cost that was bothering her.

To break the tension, Edna turned to Paula. "So did you ever have aspirations to paint?"

Paula took a good-sized swig of tea and swished it around her teeth like mouthwash, then answered the question. "No. My father was an attorney, and his father before that. It was pretty much written in stone that I would study law." She rolled her eyes, but I think she was proud to be a lawyer. "What about you, Edna?" she asked. "Do you have any artistic abilities?"

Edna crinkled her forehead. "I can't draw. My sister gave me art supplies for my birthday, and I tried to paint my cat Cecily." She put her hands over her eyes. "She wound up looking like a crocodile with ears." Paula and I laughed, but Grand-mama stared in that unforgiving way of hers.

I don't know where she found the courage, but Edna took a deep breath and dared to say, "Anyway, just so you know, Mrs. Gladstone would likely give lessons for butter and eggs. She'd be happier with that than cash."

My head turned on a swivel. "Really?"

"Butter and eggs…," mumbled Paula. "I suppose Mrs. Gladstone would be better than nothing. Not much, though."

Better than nothing was right. From where I sat, any lesson would be manna from heaven. I didn't care if it was Mrs. Gladstone or the abominable snowman doing the teaching.

"And you are welcome to use those paints and brushes that my sister gave me. They are nothing to write home about, but they'd be enough to get you started." She wrinkled her forehead again. "I'd be happy to be rid of them."

Baby Rebecca, who'd been napping in her crib, let out a big cry. In a way, I was relieved when Grandmama had to tend to her, because it gave me a chance to find out more about Mrs. Gladstone.

"And she would be willing to give me lessons in exchange for butter and eggs?"

"I am sure of it," said Edna. "I could drive you to Elmira—providing your parents will allow you to go."

Paula wrote something down in her book.

"You're not putting Mrs. Gladstone in your book, are you?" joked Edna.

All of a sudden, my stomach felt sick. Sick from the excitement of the sheer possibility of real art lessons, yet queasy at the thought of not being allowed to go. Everything jumbled together and I felt like I was going to explode.

Right at that moment, my parents and brother arrived home. All Isaiah could drum up was a quick "Hello," before diving right into the topic of cookies. He threw his jacket onto the rack, quickly washed his hands in the sink, and without even drying them, sat at the table and reached for a bun.

"Why are you so interested in rigglevake cookies?" he asked.

"This is my brother, Isaiah," I said.

"Pleased to meet you," she replied.

That was the end of the pleasantries, so he asked again, "What is the big deal with the railroad cookies?"

Without batting an eyelid, the lawyer replied, "My client, the *Mother's Best* company, is being sued for fifty million dollars."

Everyone in the room drew a breath at the same time.

"Fifty million?" said Isaiah. "Wow!"

No one else said anything. We were flabbergasted.

"And the one person in North America who can prevent that from happening," she said coolly, as if presenting a case in court, "is right here in this room."

All eyes turned to Grand-mama.

It had to be her.

CHAPTER FIVE

"I have to tell you," said Paula, as we made our way to the henhouse, "your grandmother is the equivalent of a one-woman board of investigation. Her remarks are like little darts shooting around the room." She smirked. "I had to keep jumping from side to side to avoid getting struck." Paula couldn't hold a candle to Grand-mama where the setting of moral standards was concerned, but she had it all over her in dramatics. She stopped to adjust her feet inside the rubber boots that we had loaned her. "These things must weigh ten pounds each," she said. I was embarrassed that she had to wear the work boots, but there was no way her New York shoes would have made it through the deep snow. I was surprised she got from Edna's car to our front door, but then again, she was on a mission. "I thought she was going to strangle me when I suggested she would have to testify in court."

Still stunned from her revelation about the fifty-million-dollar lawsuit, and feeling self-conscious about taking a woman who had visited the Metropolitan Museum of Art to our henhouse, I walked stiff-legged and cut a zigzag path through our side yard.

"I must admit," said Paula, "despite her temperament, your grandmother is quite a baker. Those rolls of hers were amazing. I had to stop myself from eating a dozen." She thought for a moment. "I can see I have my work cut out for me. There is no way she is going to let me take that recipe book to New York."

"It has been in our family for many years," I said.

"I promise to be careful with it." Her voice changed on the spot. "You do realize that I will have to present it as evidence." She paused. "You are a bright girl. And I know you are aware of what has to happen here. You're the one who can make your grandmother understand."

"Well, I—"

"I know your parents can use the money," she added. "They look worn out, they really do. I assure you that my firm would pay handsomely to have that recipe book." She shook her head in dismay. "It's your grandmother that is going to be the problem."

In spite of her vehement assurance that I possessed enough wisdom and tenacity to deal with my grandmother, I suddenly felt myself being pushed into the middle of the ring. The bell sounded, they banged their gloves together, and my work as referee between the two contenders began. I knew the match would be a long one—they were equal in strength and determination—but whether I could go the distance was very much in question.

"Anyway," continued the lawyer, "she has agreed to bake the cookies for me. That is the first step." She sighed heavily. "She refuses to be paid for it, though. She's crafty enough to realize that payment might obligate her in some way."

"You have to prove that they are crispy and chewy at the same time, right?" My mind had bounced back and forth so many times between *Starry Night* and rigglevake cookies that I wasn't sure if I had the facts of the lawsuit straight.

"Yes," said Paula. "As I tried to explain to your grandmother and parents, my client is being sued because they brought cookies to market that were advertised as having two textures, but *Baker's Pride*, their rival, claims to have a patent on that formula."

"So, if they have a patent, it means no one else can sell cookies like that?"

"Correct. However, no one can put a patent on a cookie that has been around as long as your rigglevakes have. That's the key to our case," she explained. "I tell you, we searched every cookbook on the planet to find a cookie that uses these two types of dough, and your grandmother's recipe was the only one out there."

"So if you presented Grand-mama's little black book in court, *Baker's Pride* would not be able to sue." I thought for a moment. "If the cookies really are crispy and chewy at the same time."

"They are...aren't they?"

"Sometimes." It had been my experience that every time I baked a cookie—any kind of cookie—it came out different. "When you bake something, doesn't it come out different every time?"

"I've never baked in my life."

"Oh," I said. Her remark came as a surprise to me. Mennonite girls start separating egg whites around the age of five, and by seven can turn out a fairly decent pan of brownies.

"It doesn't matter," said Paula. "I will watch your grandmother do it." She looked me square in the eye, and I had the feeling she could see straight through me. "But I will need that recipe book."

My mother and father, tired from working all day at the barn raising, had sent me to fetch eggs. Edna stayed inside to help get things ready for the test-baking. I couldn't figure out why Paula was so eager to join me; I assumed squawking chickens were one step up from Grand-mama in her estimation. Looking back, with the clear-sightedness that time so often brings, I know now that she wanted to talk to me alone. I was the one she was betting on.

"My grandmother is very conservative," I said. "But really, everyone in the Old Order is that way."

"That's putting it mildly," said the lawyer. "No cars, no lights, no television, no radio—I don't know how you stand it. Truly, I don't." She paused for a moment. "Why do you put yourself through such inconvenience?"

I had no answer. It never seemed inconvenient to me.

With Topper leading the way, Paula followed me down the lane between the forest and big bank barn, where we kept Della and our cows, and past the smoke house to a smaller barn inside a large fenced area.

"Your dog won't chase the chickens?" she asked.

"No, he's well behaved," I said. As I did, it occurred to me that she must be thinking that Mennonite dogs, like Mennonite children, are far too obedient for their own good. I quickly added, "Most of the time, anyway."

We entered the brooder house to a loud *SQUAWK*, then not so loudly, *squawk*, *squawk*, *squawk*, and Paula stopped in her tracks when the chickens started flying off their perches and jumping down from the rafters. I checked the dropping boards and was relieved that they didn't look too dirty. It was Isaiah's job to clean off the manure, and he didn't always get around to it, but this time I was lucky.

Paula put her hands over her head and shut her eyes.

"Do they bite?"

"No," I said, letting out a little laugh. "Chickens don't have teeth."

"Oh," said Paula, opening one eye.

"They peck, though," I said.

"I'll wait at the door. That way I can escape if they come after me." Paula took that little notepad of hers out of her pocket. It had a pen stuck in the side coils. I couldn't imagine what she'd ever find to record about our henhouse.

"Did you want me to tell you about chickens?" I asked her.

"I'm not sure," she confessed. "By the time I get back to the office, they expect me to know everything there is to know about rigglevake cookies, and that includes every ingredient and where it came from. So I suppose chickens are part of it all." She shrugged. "How many eggs do these things lay, anyway?"

"An average Leghorn will produce more than two hundred eggs per year," I replied. I knew that from a school essay I wrote. Paula put it down in her book, but I somehow doubted that it would ever come up in court.

While I checked the laying boxes, Paula kicked around at the straw under her feet. Every time a chicken would squawk, she'd cover her ears and squint. I could tell she didn't like them. "You have never been on a farm, have you?" I asked.

"No," said Paula. "I am not the farm type. In fact, any place from which you can't see the Manhattan skyline with the naked eye is too rural for me." Then she added, "I had a friend once who decided to escape the claws of civilization," she said. "But after a month in the boondocks she started welcoming visits from anyone. Even a vacuum-cleaner salesman banging at the door was a welcome sight."

The lawyer scowled when a chicken jumped down and perched on her shoulder. I quickly shooed it off, but some tiny feathers were left on her fancy coat. I was going to brush them away but thought better of it. I figured what she didn't know wouldn't hurt her. "Sorry," I said. "You know, I could have done this myself. You didn't have to come out here."

"Don't worry about it." Paula thought for a moment, then added, "I must admit that gathering eggs, except on Easter morning, has definitely never been on my to-do list."

"Stand back, all of you," Grand-mama commanded us through clenched teeth. Hands covered with flour, she stood at the long baking table, rolling out two giant circles of dark and light dough. My brother tried to break off a piece of the dark one, but she slapped his hand with the edge of the pin. "Sit down, Isaiah," she said. "If everyone...." She looked directly at Paula. "If everyone is so determined to see if these cookies are— what did you say? Crispy and chewy?"

"That's right, Clara," said Edna.

The lawyer did a double-take. I don't think she realized my grandmother had a first name. I am sure she didn't count on ever being invited to use it, but likely felt a tad relieved to know she had one, and was therefore human, like the rest of us.

My grandmother kept the now-infamous black-covered notebook beside her. The handwriting on its pages had faded with time, and with so many splats of batter and fat strewn throughout, it was hard to believe that so much money was resting on its contents. The lawyer never took her eyes off that little book. In fact, her gaze was so intense, I had the distinct feeling that given the opportunity (and better driving conditions) she would have snatched it from my grandmother's grip and made a mad dash to the airport. She shuddered every time my grandmother picked it up with her floury hands. We didn't make those cookies very often, so Grand-mama wanted to check to be certain she was getting the two types of dough right. At one point, when she ran her finger down the list to be sure she hadn't missed an ingredient, Paula covered her eyes, just like she did in the henhouse. I suppose with fifty million dollars riding on that recipe, she didn't want it obscured by a greasy fingerprint.

"The key to the difference," said Grand-mama as she worked, "is that whereas one part uses eggs, the other uses molasses."

Paula scribbled down her every word.

"I like gumdrop cookies better," said Sarah, watching from the sidelines.

"I do, too," said Isaiah. "Railroad cookies look fancy, but don't taste any different from ordinary rounds."

I agreed with my brother. Other than the fact that the two colors swirled together like a spiral, the cookies seemed normal in every way.

"Eggs will keep a batter crispy," explained my mother, "so the fact that the dark part has no eggs is probably why it stays rather soft."

"Uh huh, uh huh…." The lawyer's hand moved swiftly, like she was taking shorthand.

"Why didn't you bake them yourself?" asked Isaiah.

"Son!" scolded my father.

"Well, I didn't mean…."

"That's okay," said Paula. "Around here, you women are taught to bake before you learn to walk. I can't even boil water."

"Goodness!" exclaimed Grand-mama. She stopped her work for a moment, and I was sure she was just about to give one of her lectures on the proper role of women. She must have thought better of it—maybe because Edna was there, and she liked Edna—because she held her tongue and resumed her task of cookie-baking without saying a word. She carefully placed one circle of dough upon the other, rolled it up into a tube, and sliced off rounds.

"How long do you bake these things for?" asked Paula, gesturing at the unbaked cookies with her pen.

"About ten minutes," said Grand-mama. "And be sure to keep the fire at an even temperature."

"The fire?" That stumped the lawyer. She bit the end of her pen. "What temperature is a fire?"

"I have no idea."

My grandmother said she had no idea, but she knew. She was just being difficult.

"Three hundred and fifty degrees," said Edna.

Paula peered into the oven as Grand-mama slid the pan inside. The lawyer then walked slowly away, and backwards, taking only baby steps and sitting down softly when she returned to her place at the table.

"It's not a soufflé," sniffed Grand-mama.

"Cookies don't sink the way a cake does," I explained. "But I have burned quite a few."

"She has," agreed my brother. "Either that or they come out raw in the middle."

"Beth is learning to be quite a good baker," said my mother.

"Am I too, Mama? Am I a good baker?" Sarah chimed in.

My mother smiled and rubbed the top of her head. Then she heard the baby crying from her crib. The smell of the cookies baking likely roused her from her sleep.

"Young Sarah helped her mama make jelly muffins last week," said my father. That made my sister smile.

"Have you really never made anything?" I asked Paula. "Not even when you were little?"

"No," she said. "I asked for an Easy-Bake Oven for my birthday once, but I got a set of law books instead."

The only one who laughed was Edna. The rest of us weren't sure what she was talking about. "And I suppose you watched Perry Mason instead of cartoons?" Edna was smiling.

"Perry Mason?" I wondered.

"Oh, he was a lawyer on a television program," said Edna. She winked at me. "I am guessing you don't know what an Easy-Bake Oven is either?"

My mother spoke up. "That's an electric oven. You can just turn a dial to whatever temperature you like."

Paula laughed out loud, and I felt embarrassed for

my mother, even though I thought, too, that it must be a cook stove that ran on hydro.

Edna broke in. "It's just a silly toy. Not something you would ever want, because you can't turn out anything but a sickly sweet cupcake. The box it comes in probably tastes better than what you can make in those things."

"What about your mother?" I asked Paula. "Didn't she bake?"

"No," replied the lawyer. "One Christmas she made fruitcakes that were so hard, everyone was shocked to find that they hadn't been wrapped in the pan after all." She paused to think for a moment. "You people celebrate Christmas in January, right?"

My grandmother shook her head in disbelief. "We're not Ukrainian."

Edna interjected again, but I think she was running out of diversion subjects because all she could muster was, "Your grandmother, now she must have baked."

"I can't remember, but she did do a lot of needlework. She tried to teach me how to knit a sweater once, but when I finished, the waistline was somewhere around my knees."

Isaiah and I laughed at the same time, and it must

have been loud, because the baby started to cry again. Mama picked her up and sat her in her highchair at the table. Paula was seated directly beside her and shifted her chair away when the baby started playing with her hair. Then she tapped her pen on the table while simultaneously drumming her right foot to the same beat. The ten minutes that those cookies baked were the longest in history, and even my father felt the tension. Ordinarily, he'd be working in the barn, or gathering wood, or feeding Della. He wasn't one to hang around the kitchen, at least not until it was time to eat. Like all of us, he was curious to see the results.

Grand-mama put on her big red oven mitts, and the boxing image returned to haunt me. I was reminded of the horrible fact that Paula fully expected me to be on her side of the ring. I knew a day would come when she would ask me to convince my family to turn over the recipe book.

All eyes were on my grandmother as she lifted the cookies off the pan, one by one, and placed them onto a cooling rack.

"Can't tell if they're crispy and chewy yet," she said. "They must be completely cool."

Paula wrote that down.

We waited patiently for the unveiling.

After another ten minutes had elapsed—Grand-mama decided upon the cooling time, even though all the recipe said was "allow to stand"—everyone reached for a cookie.

CHAPTER SIX

Just as I was about to take that fateful bite—fateful because if they weren't crispy and chewy, it was going to cost Paula's client fifty million dollars—there was a knock at the door. One of those big, loud, single knocks that usually herald the arrival of someone significant, like the preacher, who knows he is important. The people who feel a bit sheepish because they are coming with no good reason other than to chat or borrow a piece of equipment usually go with a series of small *tap-tap-tap*s.

I put my cookie down, and so did my mother. She and I, together with Topper, went through the hall to answer the door. Because whomever it was didn't come to the side entrance, we knew right away that he or she was not a frequent visitor. "I wonder who that could be?" said Mama.

I shrugged as I pulled open the heavy oak door.

I was surprised to see my friend Ann Weber standing there. And not with her grandfather but with her mother, whom I knew, and a tall man who I had never seen before in my life. The three of them were covered in snow. Not the nice, soft, flaky kind, but the hard pellet type that doesn't look threatening but can be as penetrating as a fire hose. I glanced over their shoulders and out to the lane to see if they had come in Ann's family cutter, but they had not. There was a huge, long car parked out there, the kind a wealthy person would drive.

"Come in, come in, that wind is freezing," said my mother. "Down Topper," she scolded, when he jumped up onto the man's coat. Then he sniffed at a bag that Ann's mother was carrying. I wondered what was inside.

"Hello, Livvy," said Mrs. Weber.

"Hello, Malinda," returned my mother. As in most cases where you don't know what to say, weather is always the best bet. "I believe we are in for a treacherous storm. If it gets even a few degrees milder, that snow will turn to ice rain."

"We're sorry to come unannounced," said the man, "but—well, uh—you people don't have phones."

When he called us "you people," it made me feel like I was from Mars. At least my mother didn't start talking about squirrel's tails and pine cones when she discussed the weather.

By that time, Edna, Paula, and my grandmother had joined us by the door to see who had come to call.

Edna recognized the man right away.

"Sid Ross…I didn't expect to see you again. Not so soon, anyway." She smiled at Mrs. Weber and brushed snow from Ann's collar. "So, it looks like you found someone to bake the rigglevake cookies for you."

I wonder why this man wants to bake rigglevakes? I asked myself.

Edna must have read my mind—and my mother's too, by the puzzled look she had—because she quickly explained. "Mr. Ross is the attorney for the *Baker's Pride* company."

Paula's face turned to stone. She began to take shorter breaths and frowned just like when the chicken had perched on her shoulder. Then she felt around the inside pocket of her blazer and exhumed an antacid that looked as if it had been rolling around in there for several months. I figured it was part of an emergency stash for those times when she didn't have her purse with her.

"I see," said Paula, rubbing lint from the pill, then tossing it into her mouth. "Come to spy, did you?" she added. I wondered if her knife-edged remark would startle my mother, but I think she was still processing the fact that a second lawyer was standing in our hallway, and that he, too, was interested in our cookies. And Grand-mama, well, she rather enjoyed the confrontation.

"You must be Miss Logan," said the tall lawyer, extending his hand. Paula did the same, but her arm was so limp, you'd think that Sid Ross was a surgeon looking to take her pulse before wheeling her into the operating room.

By that time, my father and brother had joined the group, and everyone was introduced to everyone. Then my mother invited the newcomers to join us back in the kitchen. Paula didn't like that idea at all.

"That's not going to happen." She swelled her nostrils and drew in her lips. "Our research is strictly for my client, and I don't want—"

"Research!" Grand-mama was incensed. Her nostrils swelled, too. "This is my home, not some laboratory, and those are my cookies, and if I want to share them with Mrs. Weber and her daughter, then I will do it!" She sniffed. "This is why I refused your money!"

My parents exchanged glances in that same way they did the first time payment was mentioned. I imagined both of them had a devil on their shoulder, whispering in their ear about how that extra cash would have paid for new roofing shingles.

"With all due respect," said Mr. Ross, addressing himself to Paula in particular, "it is in both our best interests to determine the texture of the cookies."

Paula turned to Edna. "I gather that you were asked to bake cookies for his law firm as well?"

"I was," said Edna. She looked guiltily out the front door, and I wondered if she was thinking about making a run for it. "But since you asked me first, I advised Mr. Ross to find another Mennonite woman in the area to help him." She put her arm around Ann. "The Weber family are good cooks. I suggested he ask them."

Mrs. Weber's voice cracked when she spoke. "I didn't realize we'd be put at odds with our neighbors. I never would have—"

"We're not at odds," said my mother, and my father agreed.

"Not at all, Malinda," he said. "Let's go back to the kitchen, shall we? Let's see how the cookies turned out."

We returned to the long pine table. The newcomers hung their coats and hats on the backs of chairs, and then everyone sat down and stared at each other. It was getting dark outside, and by the light of the sputtering kerosene lamps, it was just like the reading of a will, or maybe one of those séances that I'd learned about in Victorian novels. My skin drew tight and I had a gulpy feeling in my throat.

"We haven't baked our cookies yet," admitted Ann. "We came to see you first."

"I know how to do it," said Mrs. Weber, "but I told Mr. Ross it would be better if Clara was present, to be absolutely sure I did it correctly, since it is her recipe, after all." Her voice cracked again. "It's not like I make those every day."

"It is not my recipe," protested Grand-mama. "It was passed down from generation to generation for everyone to use."

There was a moment of silence. The Mennonites amongst us were likely having pious thoughts about how no one can really own anything in this life, whereas the lawyers were probably trying to figure out how my grandmother's statement about it not being her recipe might benefit their court case. Then again, maybe no one was thinking much of anything.

Ann spoke up. "We brought all the ingredients. Just not the eggs because they'd break." She pointed to the mysterious bag.

"Can we try one yet?" asked my brother. "I've never waited so long to eat a cookie in my life."

"I like gumdrop cookies better." My sister was still pushing for her favorites.

Grand-mama put out three more plates and made sure we all had a rigglevake in front of us. I even gave one to Topper, which he ate whole.

I was about to say, *May the best man win*, but thought better of it. Paula was not a man, there was fifty million riding on it, and for the two cookie companies, the whole thing was not some jolly affair. It was tantamount to war.

Mr. Ross took one bite, and immediately proclaimed, "No...no, this is just like any other cookie." He didn't give the whole crispy and chewy thing a chance. His mouth was full of crumbs, and he mumbled something that sounded like, "It's rust mrispy, rike any." He swallowed. "Crispy, that's what they are. Not chewy at all." He threw down the almost-untouched cookie, and for him, the case was closed.

"You're out of your mind. These cookies are definitely chewy in the darker parts," said Paula. "Absolutely and unequivocally." She stood up and brushed crumbs from her lap. I wasn't sure what *unequivocally* meant, but everyone in the room got the message: she was ready to fight and would fight to the bitter end.

"I think they are chewy in the middle, but rather crisp on the edge," offered my father, and my mother nodded in agreement.

"I think they are soft all the way through," said Isaiah, and Mr. Ross held up his right thumb, gesturing as if to applaud my brother for his good judgment.

"You said they were crispy, Mr. Ross," said Paula. She didn't preface it with "Aha! Caught you!" but the sentiment was there.

"Can we make gumdrop cookies next?" Sarah was relentless. She hadn't even bitten into her rigglevake yet.

"I think these cookies do have two different textures all right," said Edna, taking another bite. "I am just not sure if 'crispy' and 'chewy' are the right adjectives."

"Adjectives be damned," hollered Paula. There was a collective gasp, and she caught herself. "I'm sorry," she said, and I think she was going to cross her chest the way Catholics do, but after the Ukrainian remark, she couldn't trust her knowledge of religious dates and practices.

All eyes fell to Grand-mama.

"I will bet you agree with me, don't you Mrs. Betzner?" said Mr. Ross. His voice was overly sweet. It was a wonder he didn't add, *you dear little woman you*. Lawyers, it would seem, are very good at getting people to say exactly what they need them to say.

Grand-mama didn't fall for any of it.

"I don't bet," said my grandmother. "The evils of gambling can put down roots in shallow ground." According to our preacher, Mennonites are supposed to be content, self-sufficient, pacifist, and unassuming. Grand-mama had the first three of those mastered.

"Well, you're the cook, what do you say?" said Paula, waving her hand imperiously, as if to hasten my grandmother's response.

That gesture didn't sit well with Grand-mama.

"I'll not be provoked."

The tension in the room was at a peak, so Edna intervened. "I think it's time we leave the Betzners to themselves," she said. "They've been working all day at the barn raising, and it is well past their supper time." She stood up and pushed her chair back into the table. "Paula, we will have to bake these ourselves, and more than once, to come to a full analysis. The Betzner family has been good enough to show us how it is done, and we cannot ask for any more than that."

My sister was getting tired and had nodded off more than once. And I saw Isaiah fight back a yawn.

Mrs. Weber rose, and helped Ann into her coat. "We do have to be getting back home," she said. "That storm is beginning to pick up tempo." She picked up her bag of ingredients. I wasn't sure if she was going to bake for Mr. Ross or not, now that his mind was made up. Either way, we'd all had enough cookie tasting for one night.

"It is indeed," said Edna, "and I don't want to be driving in it, even if I am just down the road. They are predicting a temperature rise, and if it does, we'll be dealing with ice."

Paula was still adamant that the cookies were crispy and chewy, and started picking them off the cooling rack and bending them to prove her point. "Now if the dark part was crispy, they would not be pliable like this."

Edna implored her with every known signal that it was time to leave.

"Oh, all right," she said. "But I can tell you right now, Mr. Ross, that the Betzners are my witnesses, not yours. I don't care how many other people in this area you find to bake cookies for you, Grandmother Betzner and her little black book will be used for the purpose of the defense in this case."

"We'll see about that," said Mr. Ross calmly, reaching for his hat and scarf.

"You are purposely trying to aggravate me," declared Paula.

"We'll see about what?" said Grand-mama. I followed her gaze to the recipe book, which was still sitting next to the baking table. "I won't set foot in court. I won't be testifying for any of you."

"He's antagonizing me," repeated Paula.

"I will not testify!" My grandmother raised her voice. "And I will not be lured by offers of money, no matter how much." She looked daggers at both lawyers. "Our heritage is not for sale!"

I remembered someone once told me that a good way to get someone to tell the truth was to get them mad at you. I decided that lawyers, like grandmothers, used confrontation as a way to find out what they wanted to know.

My friend Ann looked as if she was about to sob.

"You're upsetting the children," said Edna. "It's time we leave."

My father held open the door while the visitors filed out. Edna waited in her car while Paula gathered samples of the ingredients we used (she even took an egg) and some of the cookies, too. She seemed to be going about this in a sort of slow motion; I think she was stalling to be sure the other lawyer didn't come back and try to get the black book from my grandmother.

There wasn't a snowball's chance in the wood fire of that ever happening.

Paula wasn't a quitter though.

"My firm would be willing to pay a lot of money for the loan of that book, Mrs. Betzner."

"No."

Grand-mama moved swiftly to her baking table and seized the recipe book. For the first time ever, she did not return it to its usual place. Like a dog with a bone, she shuffled around the kitchen, trying to find a safe place to hide it. She finally decided upon the oak cupboard near the back door. She used her step stool to reach the top shelf. My father kept his hat up there—the one he wore for special—and his kid leather gloves. Those he used when driving the cutter to church because they were of a higher quality than his usual ones and gripped the reins perfectly. "There now," said my grandmother, "that will put an end to all this foolishness." I guess she was thinking "out of sight, out of mind," but I don't think it did much to assuage either one of the lawyer's thirst to get their hands on the black-covered notebook.

Paula left with a half-eaten cookie in her hand and walked crabwise through the pelting snow, leaving a trail of crumbs behind her, just like in Hansel and Gretel. Even as she got into Edna's car, I could hear her mumbling something about baking them in an electric oven because maybe the wood fire dried out the product too much. Then I heard the sound of their wheels spinning on an icy patch. The lawyer's car had spun also, but both vehicles made it out eventually. By the time I'd closed the door, only Topper and I were left in the hallway. He was licking up the crumbs. "So, what do you think? Are they crispy and chewy?"

He let out a bark, and I rubbed his back.

Like Topper, I didn't really care too much about rigglevake cookies. Little did I know that those biscuits, and the war that was generated because of a patent for dough and storage-stable texture variability, would change the course of my life in ways that I never could have imagined.

CHAPTER SEVEN

I was downstairs, behind the bank-vault-like door of the root cellar, when I heard a commotion above me. I knew someone had come to call because Topper was barking, and there was the sound of feet shuffling over my head. I hurried up to the kitchen, a pound of butter in my hand, and spotted a huge bouquet of red and white azaleas. They'd come from a commercial florist because there was shiny wrap all over the pot and cellophane to cover the blooms. I couldn't remember any other time that flowers had been delivered to us. We all stood around in a circle, peering at the display like it was a foundling left on the doorstep.

"Flowers in the dead of winter," said my grandmother with a sigh that, if translated, meant something akin to *What has this world come to?* She didn't believe in anything out of season unless it was cured, canned, or in a crock.

My mother felt different. "I know, aren't they beautiful?"

She loved flowers, and in the summer, there was always a bouquet on our table. In the early spring, it would consist of pussy willows and the first wildflowers that popped up out of the snow. In May, she would fill a vase with twigs of blossoms from the old pear tree. From her garden, she would cut daffodils and snow-drops and tulips. And of course, her beloved roses. Oh, how Mama loved those blooms. She had a rose garden that looked and smelled the way I think heaven must. She had white roses, pink roses, yellow roses, and many mixtures thereof—but her favorite were the delicate, peach-colored ones. I'd have to say that what she cherished most in life, other than her family, was that garden. I often watched her from my window at daybreak; she'd be digging in the earth around her flowers, admiring their beauty. I suppose it was a peaceful time for her, before the day began, to be alone with her thoughts.

Mama turned the pot around to examine the blooms and unpinned a tag from where it was attached to the foil.

"What does it say?" my brother asked.

"To the Betzners…many thanks for your hospitality," she read. "And it is signed by Sid Ross, the lawyer, on behalf of his firm."

Well, I said to myself, *it could have been worse. It could have said "See you in court."*

"Bribery!" hissed Grand-mama. "The man won't take no for an answer."

"I think they are pretty," chortled my sister, pulling off a bloom and tucking it into her hair.

"Look at that, will you?" My grandmother pointed to Sarah's head. Mennonites are not supposed to wear jewelry or any embellishments, so my sister's attempt at looking beautiful, however meager it might have been, was viewed by my grandmother as one giant step in the wrong direction. Mama pulled it from behind her ear and tried to stuff it back into the bouquet, but it dropped into her coffee. She then took it out with a spoon and set it on her plate.

"I hope this Mr. Ross doesn't think we can be bought," said my father, buttering a thick slice of freshly baked bread.

"I don't care what the man thinks," said Grand-mama, her eyes flashing towards where she'd hidden the little recipe book atop the oak cupboard. "They can fight their cookie war all by themselves. We are not about to take part."

Mama dropped her gaze to the floor. "It would have been nice to have a little extra money, though."

"Livvy!" said Grand-mama. "If we took even a few dollars from those wicked lawyers, they'd say we owed them something. Then we'd be in trouble."

"It wasn't just a few dollars," replied my father. "Paula Logan implied that we would be paid off very well." He stopped. "But I agree that we can't accept any compensation. It could put us in a position to be forced into court."

"Your father would never have allowed any of this," said Grand-mama. She rarely spoke of my grandfather, and when she did it was usually to summon his authority on something or frighten us into submission. "He wouldn't allow any lawyer to push him around, I know that much."

My brother mumbled something. He was eating a pancake at the time, so I couldn't tell exactly what he was saying, but it was clear that he, too, wanted nothing to do with the world of corporate espionage no matter how much of an adventure it might be. Unlike myself, Isaiah was quite content with the status quo. I felt like an imposter because for some reason I was compelled to nod my head in agreement, when all the while, I was finding the whole thing exciting. And meeting Paula Logan, a person who had actually been to see so many famous paintings—well, that had made my life complete.

Maybe as a way of being honest about my feelings, or maybe because I thought the flowers, and the conversation they provoked, would be a good diversion for my grandmother's wrath, I suddenly found myself with enough courage to bring up the topic of art lessons.

"Edna says there's a woman, Mrs. Gladstone is her name, and she teaches art. It wouldn't cost anything. She would take butter and eggs for payment."

Silence.

All I could hear was the baby gurgling, my brother swallowing food, and Topper's foot hitting the floor as he scratched his side quarters.

"Edna could drive me there and back. She doesn't mind. In fact, she really wants to do it. And like I said, it wouldn't cost anything. Edna has some paints and brushes that she doesn't want." My hopes soared high, but were quickly dashed with a simple, but final word from my father.

"No."

"But—"

"I said no, Beth." He reached for some syrup and poured a little pond of it onto his plate, then lifted two pancakes and floated them on top. "Anyway, the doctor told you that you should be very careful when it comes to your wrist. I don't think it's a good idea to be using it for anything unnecessary like that."

Unnecessary.

It doesn't feel unnecessary to me.

I hung my head.

"Don't sulk," said Grand-mama, but the tone of her voice was so severe, my mother stepped in to soften things a little.

"Now dear, you know that we are not encouraged to hang paintings. Don't you remember what the preacher said about it? He told us—"

"What about Peter Etril Snyder? And Agatha Loewen Duerksen Schmidt? They are both Mennonites, and they are both artists."

"Oh, not that again!" My grandmother threw up her arms.

"Not what again?" asked Isaiah.

"They paint scenes of our heritage. Really, they do." Everyone just sort of stared at me, blankly. I couldn't put my sentences together in any meaningful way.

I wished at that moment that I had the money to hire Paula to defend me. Or Sid Ross. Even he would do.

I wanted to say so much more about how important it all was to me, but nothing I said was strong enough. Nothing really expressed what I felt inside. I reckoned that, ultimately, the less I said the better. And the more likely that my future would include lessons with Mrs. Gladstone. Like a coiled spring of willpower, I bit my tongue.

"Eat your oatmeal," said my father.

"But—"

"I told you to eat your breakfast." There was a definite tone to his voice, so I gave up the topic of art lessons. I decided that I would try again, maybe in a few days. Then I concluded that it was a good time to bring up something else that I wanted. I figured it would be difficult for my parents to turn me down twice within a matter of minutes.

"May I go to Edna's after school today to watch her and Paula bake the rigglevake cookies?"

"Were you invited?" asked my mother.

"She was," said my grandmother. "That Logan woman wants to try making them for herself. I suppose she'll be asked to do it for the team of lawyers, if you can imagine such nonsense." She grimaced.

"And Edna wants to take her through the covered bridge before she goes back to New York," I added.

"She really should see it," said my mother.

"I wish we could take her for a ride in our sleigh before she leaves." I wasn't trying to be difficult. I honestly felt that Paula would really enjoy it.

"Oh, good heavens," said Grand-mama. "I already told this child that we didn't have time for foolish escapades. She just won't listen to a word I say anymore."

My father took a sip of his coffee and looked me in the eye. "Young lady, you are acting particularly defiant this morning. Is something bothering you?"

I said nothing. I didn't know what to say. I turned to face Mama, perhaps in an attempt to tug on her heartstrings, or appeal to her motherly instincts. I said nothing but pleaded with my eyes.

"I think it is okay to visit Edna today," she said, "just as long as she drives you home." She glanced out the window. "I think it will be milder as the day progresses."

"That could be worse," was my grandmother's cheery response. "We're in for ice rain."

"How are we getting to the Martins' place?" asked Isaiah.

I had forgotten all about the barn raising.

"The Webers are taking us with them. They're driving up to Floradale with their team of horses and the full-sized sleigh," said my father. "Other than a few extra hammers, we won't be having to carry tools. The Martins have the equipment right there." He reached for another slice of bread, then addressed Isaiah. "We'll need you at the sawmill, son, to help cut boards. The women will be at the main house finishing up the quilt."

"It's a beauty," said my mother. "It will bring in enough money for all the hardware. And the paint, too."

"In some ways," said my grandmother, "it's a good thing that Beth will be with Edna this afternoon, with all of us gone."

"You're going to the quilting?" I asked her.

"Yes, and Sarah is coming with us."

"I don't have to go to school?" said Sarah with a huge grin. It was the same length as my frown, only turned the other way around.

"Your teacher will be at the quilting. No classes for your grade today."

Lucky Sarah, I said to myself.

"Why do I have to go to school?" I asked, although

I would rather go to Edna's than to the quilting. My response must have been a knee-jerk reaction to the fact that when one's brother and sister are off the hook as far as school is concerned, everyone should be. Anyway, no one gave me an answer, so I didn't keep it going. I was happy to have a chance to talk with Paula Logan again. I was in for a great day ahead.

Or so I thought.

CHAPTER EIGHT

"You got flowers, too?" I asked Edna. I noticed the azaleas as soon as I entered her kitchen. Her cats, Cecily and Willie, greeted me with big "meows" and both wanted petting, so I bent over to rub their heads, then pulled off my boots. I loved visiting the cozy little cottage where Edna lived on Sunfish Lake. Maybe because there were so many tall trees surrounding her home, the smell of pine always tingled my nose as I made it up the long path to her door. Cardinals, blue jays, and chickadees fought for space at her feeders, and from time to time, one of her cats would jump into the windowsill to watch the show. It was a home away from home for me; I felt as safe as I did in our house, and yet there was an air of sophistication about her place, maybe because Edna's published books lined the shelf and she had had so many famous people visit her there. As a Mennonite, I wasn't supposed to feel self-important, but I will admit that I did feel proud to be her friend.

Edna took my coat and hat and shook them out over the doormat. "That rain is really coming down," she said. When she didn't mention the azaleas, I got to thinking that maybe I shouldn't have divulged the fact that we had been sent a bouquet from Sid Ross and his firm.

"Inducement," said Paula, voicing her displeasure. "Sheer and utter bribery. Disgraceful." The lawyer was visibly upset. Where Edna was a sort of go-between for both sides of the battle, Paula looked upon Grand-mama as her star witness. I suppose she was worried that my parents and grandmother might be cajoled into testifying on behalf of *Baker's Pride*. I knew that wouldn't happen. Mennonites never wavered in their religious convictions, and no amount of coercion would ever change that reality.

"Malinda Weber got a bouquet of azaleas too," said Edna. "And you will laugh when you hear this, Beth— Sid Ross sent her a Cuisinart!"

"A what?"

"It's a machine that kneads dough and slices vege-tables, and a million other things," explained Edna. "A sort of mixer."

A sort of mixer?

Kneads dough?

"But it won't do Mrs. Weber any good. It runs on hydro," added Paula. "And you people don't like elec-tricity for some reason. If I live to be a hundred years old, I will never understand why."

Edna gave her a dirty look. "You could sharpen knives on that tongue of yours."

Paula shrugged. "I wonder what she'll do with the Cuisinart?" she asked.

"I wouldn't hazard a guess," said Edna. "Maybe she'll store something in it. Flour or sugar. Buttons. I don't know."

"These people are living in another world!" the law-yer exclaimed. "We've landed on the moon, for Pete's sake, and around here, they're not even allowed a light bulb."

I felt embarrassed about the way we live. I knew that it would be impossible to understand—at that point in my life, I don't think I understood it myself. But Edna seemed to and managed to come up with an explanation for me.

"My Mennonite friends choose to live a simple, self-sufficient existence, Paula." She put an arm around me. "When one depends upon amenities, one puts their faith in someone, or something, other than themselves," she said.

I thought her explanation sounded pretty good—as good as I'd ever heard—but Paula was not convinced. "Kerosene lamps, for instance," she proclaimed. "What is the point? What is there to gain?" It felt like I was being tried for a crime I committed while sleepwalking.

Edna, for the defense, said, "The light from a lantern makes a woman look beautiful."

Sure, until her eyelashes get singed off, I thought to myself. It had happened to me more than once.

"And those early morning chores?" continued Paula. "You people create misery for yourselves." She sneered. "An alarm at four a.m. wouldn't wake me up," she said. "It would produce shock."

Edna fought back a smile but remained determined to get the lawyer to understand her point of view. "I want you to read an article I wrote many years ago." She opened up a cabinet door and pulled out a magazine. "It was a feature article in *Maclean's* that came out way back in nineteen fifty."

"Do I have to?" said Paula petulantly, like Edna

had just ordered her to finish eating her brussels sprouts. Then she looked shifty-eyed and said, "I'll read it later."

The title of the article was "How to Live Without Wars and Wedding Rings," and Edna was quite proud of it. "It won the Canadian Women's Press Club Award," she told us. Then she smiled at me. "Your grandmother allowed me to stay with her and her husband for a week. That's how I was able to write it."

"My father must have been there, too," I said.

"He was about ten or eleven, I'd say. Such a polite little boy, always doing chores."

Oh no, I thought, *another well-mannered Mennonite child. Paula must be ready to gag.*

Edna turned to the lawyer. "There were about twenty-five hundred members in the Old Order then. I don't think the numbers are any different now."

"What's wrong with wedding rings?" asked Paula.

"Jewelry of any kind is not condoned," replied Edna. "Simplicity is the key," she added.

I read from her article out loud. She wrote about our home, our wonderful bank barn, and the hills and fields that surround us. Her description of the snowy white blossoms on our fruit trees, and the daffodils that line our fence, made me realize why I wanted to become an artist—why I wanted to express the beauty of that landscape.

"Gosh," said Edna. "It seems like yesterday I wrote those words."

"Might as well have been," quipped Paula. "Not much changes around here." She wasn't trying to be nasty, she was still in a bad mood over the rival legal firm sending flowers and a Cuisinart.

"What's so great about change?" asked Edna, patting Cecily's back. When Willie went to rub on Paula's leg, she crossed it in the other direction to prevent the cat from touching her. I must have made a face because she mumbled something about the fur sticking to her nylons, but I think she'd have felt the same way about the cats if she was dressed in long pants and thermal underwear.

"It's the wheel that makes the world go 'round." Willie gave it another try, so this time she shooed the cat away with the sole of her foot, then picked up the magazine. At first, I thought she was going to use it as a shield, but to my surprise, she started reading it. Edna stroked her cat to comfort it after being ignored.

I spotted a piece of paper and a pencil on the coffee table. "May I use these?"

"Certainly, Beth."

I began to sketch Cecily. She had jumped into Edna's lap and was nicely relaxed. While I drew, Paula talked.

"Okay, so here's a question I have…do Mennonites pay taxes?" she asked.

"Of course," said Edna.

"You wrote here that they don't accept any government benefits…that they look after their own."

"Also true."

Paula turned to me. "Your people are suckers for punishment!"

I had no argument.

"And you won't engage in combat, right?" she asked.

I was so engrossed in my drawing, I didn't respond to her question. She asked again.

"Mennonites don't believe in combat, is that correct?"

"That's right," I said, "but many serve as medics and things like that. They just won't kill another person. They won't fight in wars."

Edna smiled. "Not even cookie wars."

We both chuckled at her remark.

"Speaking of cookies," said Paula, "I was wondering, Beth, if you would help me persuade your dear Grand-mama to let me borrow her recipe book. I can't tell you what that would mean to me. It would be so helpful to my case if I could present it to a judge."

"I don't want any pressure put on the Betzner family, Paula, you know that." Edna got up, and Cecily jumped down from the chair. Because I had the main lines in place, I was able to carry on with the sketch, observing the cat from various angles. I quickly darkened those areas that were in shadow, leaving white spots for highlights in the cat's eyes, and in places where the light struck her fur.

Edna looked over my shoulder. "That is fabulous! I had no idea you could draw like that! I love it."

Just as Edna made that remark, the phone rang. Willie awoke from where he had been napping beside her chair. Paula lifted her feet into the air so neither one of the cats could rub against her. They kept trying, though, so finally she stood up.

She took the paper from my hand.

"Wow! That is really good."

"It's just a sketch. I usually take a lot more time to complete a drawing." Paula gave me back the paper, and Cecily was sitting still, so I carried on. The compliments I received from the two women gave me a confidence I hadn't really experienced before.

"The spontaneity in your strokes is extraordinary. You have a natural talent, there is no doubt about it."

I felt good inside when she said that.

"You know those lessons that you are so eager to take?" she said. "Well, I have an idea. Let's say it's one of those things where if I help you, and you help me—"

She stopped abruptly when Edna began pushing the cradle buttons on her phone up and down frantically and hollering into the mouthpiece.

"Hello? Hello, Mary? Are you there?" She clunked down the phone. "Oh, drat!" she said. "The line is gone."

"Oh, brother," said Paula.

It didn't mean much to me. We didn't have a phone at our place and relied on the old system of dropping in when you needed to talk to someone. It wasn't convenient, but it always worked.

"That was Mary from down the road. She says the Grand River is up over its banks."

"So?" Paula didn't understand why that was a problem, but I did.

"So we won't be going to see the covered bridge," I said. "Can't get anywhere near it when the river swells like that." I stood up to look out the frosted, misty window, to what could only be described as a cold, wet, and huddled landscape. "It's really coming down now." I noticed how dark it was getting outside. The sun hadn't yet set, but the sky was as black as coal.

Edna opened the door. "Well, I can see why my phone is dead." She turned on the porch light. It flickered for a moment, then begrudgingly complied, but I had the feeling it wouldn't be long before it gave up the ghost. "Well, we might as well start baking the cookies. A trip to the bridge is out of the question now."

"It's bitter as anything," said Paula, when a gust of cold air blew through the room. The rain was freezing as it hit surfaces, collecting on tree limbs and overhead wires. "I am glad we're not venturing outside. I think my blood would turn to sherbet!" She did that shifty-eyed thing again. "So, did you bring the recipe book for us to use today?"

"No," I admitted. "But it's the same as the version that was published in Edna's book. It's a direct copy."

"Which makes me wonder why you can't just use that as evidence?" asked Edna.

"Because we need to prove that the recipe in *Food That Really Schmecks* has been around for a long time."

Edna didn't reply. Instead she took another look at my sketch.

"I couldn't do that if you paid me." She started for the kitchen, then turned to me. "May I keep your drawing?" she asked.

"Sure!" I said. "But I could do better if I had more time."

"I like it just the way it is."

Edna pinned my sketch to her bulletin board, then began getting things ready for the cookie baking. I watched her take eggs from the electric refrigerator and thought to myself how much easier it was than having to walk out to the chicken barn and look underneath a hen to see if she'd obliged.

I presumed that the reason why Paula wanted to learn to bake the cookies herself was so that, once back in the States, she could demonstrate how it was done.

"Have you tried to make the rigglevake cookies yet? Or is this your first attempt?" I asked. All of a sudden, thunderous laughter came bellowing from the kitchen. I thought Edna was going to drop the bag of sugar she held in her right hand.

"Oh, she made them all right. This morning, while I was out getting groceries."

"Were they crispy and chewy at the same time?" I wondered.

"We don't know," replied Edna. "They can only be described as black rounds of charcoal that tasted the way burning rubber smells."

"I'll get it right this time," said Paula. She walked over to the window where I stood, then whispered into my ear. "If you bring the black-covered notebook to me, I can promise that your tuition will be paid for that art school in Toronto you mentioned the other day. What do you think of that?" It might as well have been Satan making the offer.

"The Ontario College of Art?"

"You're certainly talented enough. All you need is someone to pay the costs involved, right?"

My heart began to beat. Faster, faster. For a moment, I contemplated the idea.

Grand-mama has the recipes memorized. She only refers to that book on rare occasions. Now that she has hidden it on top of the oak cupboard, she may never reach for it again. Paula would only need it for a while. She could mail it back to me. Or to Edna. I know she'd be careful with it. No one would ever be the wiser.

"I can make it happen," she told me. "I don't mean right away—obviously it would be a few years from now. But you have my word that once you are ready, you will be given the opportunity of a lifetime."

Nothing came out of my mouth except a tiny, inaudible squeak.

She kept talking.

"I mean, Mrs. Gladstone isn't going to get you to the top, no way. You need to learn from professionals. You need to try out all the different mediums—oils, acrylics, pastels. Watercolors are only the beginning. The entire cost will be paid by my firm. The *entire* cost." The hydro flickered again, this time for a longer spell, and I wondered if God was trying to send me a message.

I remembered my wrist.

"I injured my right hand, and some days it really affects my work," I said softly. "Would they still allow me to enroll in the course?"

She didn't answer my question. "I think you know this is a chance you will never get again. And I assure you that my firm will not renege on their offer. This lawsuit will be going on for a couple of years, at least. It won't be brushed under the carpet, I can tell you that."

"And all you want from me is the recipe book?"

"I cannot guarantee that your grandmother will be kept from testifying, but that has nothing to do with my promise to you. I need you to convince her to allow the book to be used as evidence." She took a long, deep breath.

Edna was still bashing around in the kitchen, measuring out flour and sugar and molasses. I wanted to call for her but didn't want to look like a big baby.

"Oh, don't do it!" she yelled. At first, I thought she had overheard us talking and was giving me a piece of her mind, but in fact, she was upset over the flickering hydro. "My trees are weighted down so far that the limbs are hitting the wires out there. That's what's doing it."

"You know," said Paula, her voice suddenly becoming sweet (which made me more suspicious than ever), "it broke my heart to see you and your family at that marketplace being gawked at by tourists. It just isn't right."

"Well, it is uncomfortable at times," I said.

"You must hate it, Beth."

I thought for a moment, then replied, "I don't care if people look at me funny, but I don't like it when they stare at my mother and father." I felt tears forming in my eyes. "I don't like that at all." Some of the people who came to buy goods from my parents treated them as a source of personal entertainment.

Edna must have been standing behind me, because she overheard my remark.

"Not all tourists are like that, of course," she said. "But some of them are quite obnoxious." She gently tugged at a lock of my hair. "Beth here is proud of her Mennonite heritage, aren't you dear?"

The confusion of being offered a chance to fulfill my dreams at the same time as feeling pain over my parents being treated like circus clowns all went together in my mind. I wanted to get them out of that situation. I wished I had all the money in the world. Not to move them from their home, but just to get them away from that market.

Edna knew nothing of the temptation that had just come my way, but she could tell I was upset and muddled. She resorted to her usual technique of diversion that usually worked so well. This time it did not.

"Okay, let's get at making these cookies," she said with a big smile. "We'll follow it to the letter and see for ourselves if these things really are crispy and chewy at the same time."

Edna headed into her kitchen and got out a sifter. "Come on, Paula, I am going to show you how to measure flour."

"Remember what I said," Paula hissed into my ear. Edna was still chattering on about flour and baking, but I heard none of it.

I had been offered a new life, a dream, a wish come true.

"Your grandmother taught me how to bake bread." That brought me back down to earth. Just the word "grandmother" was enough to blow my daydreaming to bits. "I remember the first time I took her a loaf that I had baked. It was nothing like the big, golden, crusty ones that she turns out, but I didn't think it was too bad. Well, she took one look at my creation, ripped it in half, smelled it, made a terrible face, and threw it out for the pigs." Edna laughed. "She told me I had boiled the milk too long and had killed the yeast. I suppose I—"

Just as she spoke those words, there was a big bang and every light in the house went off. Everything turned to black.

The hydro was gone. And this time, it wasn't coming back.

CHAPTER NINE

"It's like something out of a Charlie Chan movie," said Paula. All I could see was her shape in the dark, moving past me like a specter.

"Charlie Chan?"

"Sure," she said. "The Chinese detective. Every movie is the same. Right when the killer is going to be unveiled, the lights go out and the person who knows the truth gets shot."

"Oh." I had never heard of Charlie Chan.

"I can't believe this is happening," said Edna. "And I can't even call the power company without a phone connection. Not that it would do any good. They won't attempt to restore hydro until the storm is over."

She stumbled into the hallway. "I have to get some light in here. As for heat, we're out of luck."

"Don't you have a fire?" I asked.

"I have a small fireplace, but no wood," said Edna. "I burned a pile of logs in January, and didn't bother stocking up," she admitted. "Serves me right...."

I heard one of the cats screech. I think Paula stepped on its tail. "Oh, shut up," she shrieked, which angered Edna.

"It's not Cecily's fault, for heaven's sake." She was clambering around in the dark trying to find matches to light the candle on her dining room table. "I don't know where I put those blasted things."

I had never heard Edna curse before, but I don't think even Grand-mama would have blamed her under the circumstances. "Beth, could you run your hands around the bottom shelf of my storage cupboard and see if anything feels like a box of matches to you?"

"What do you want me to do?" asked Paula.

"Just don't trip over my cats or step on their tails," she said. Her tone was brusque.

Edna located a flashlight, but all it produced was a circle of faint yellow light wherever she pointed it.

"It needs new batteries," she mumbled.

I got down on my hands and knees and felt around the entire cupboard. By a trial-and-error method, I finally determined that there were no matches in there. I found what I thought might be a doorstop, but it could have been a figurine. I also located a bag of potting soil, a string of Christmas lights, a weigh scale, plenty of books, and a sack of birdseed. But no matches.

"Here they are," said Edna. I heard a *scratch, scratch, scratch* and then, just like in *Genesis*, there was light. Paula was seated at the table. She was chewing on something, which I figured had to be an antacid. I could have used one myself at that point.

Edna found a few more candles, but they didn't do much to illuminate the room.

"Those things are no better than birthday candles," said Paula.

"Have you got a better idea?"

"What about your neighbors? Maybe they have some batteries," said the lawyer.

"A flashlight won't keep us from freezing to death," said Edna. "It could be days before the hydro is restored. I know from experience. Back in 'seventy-nine, it was out for a week."

"You've got to be kidding me." Paula covered her eyes with the palms of her hands. She was exasperated.

"We can go over to my place," I said. "We have lots of food and—"

The lawyer didn't let me finish my sentence. She stood up, grabbed me, and then hugged me like I'd never been hugged before. It was as if I had come to rescue her from a desert island after finding a message she'd sent out in a bottle years before. "Of course! You don't have hydro! How wonderful!" She threw both hands in the air. "You don't have hydro!"

What a switch!

At once I felt very proud of my family traditions. I stood up straight, held out my chin, and grew an inch in height. It was like someone stuffing a rag doll. "That's right. We have heat and light, and we can cook whatever we want to."

"Oh," said Edna. "That will be wonderful. I suppose your family won't mind taking us in. We're desperate."

"They aren't at home. My father and the other men are cutting boards at the sawmill in Floradale. The women are finishing up a quilt to raise funds for the paint and whatever else the Martins need." I was starting to feel cold, so I reached for my coat. "I doubt they even know there is a power outage."

"Well, what are we waiting for?" said Paula. "Let's go to Beth's place!"

Edna rolled her eyes. Any other time she might have been tempted to rub it in—the fact that the lawyer had made such a fuss about my people and their insistence upon self-reliance. But the situation was too uncomfortable for all of us. She just wanted to find a warm place where we could get something to eat and not have to sit around in the dark.

"Now you two be good, you hear?" Edna told her cats as she filled their bowls with fresh food, then blew out the candle.

"Oh, they can see in the dark for heaven's sake." I don't know if she was cold or hungry or both, but Paula wanted out of there as fast as her feet would take her.

The three of us cowered in the freezing rain as we made it out to where Edna was parked. Over the loud bashing sound of the precipitation as it hit the top of her car, I heard an owl hoot apologetically from a tall pine. I climbed into the back seat behind Edna, and Paula took the passenger seat up front. The tires spun and for a moment, I didn't think we'd even make it out of the driveway. But make it we did, and before too long, we were on the road. Everything was in darkness except for a sliver of a moon that hung quietly in the sky before us.

Edna's car skidded as she turned onto the side road near a small viaduct under which a tributary of the Grand ran its course. Even it was higher than normal, because all the creeks were carrying water away from the river. She headed slowly in the direction of the main road. Again, her wheels began to whirl. It was as though we were driving over quicksand, because she could get no traction whatsoever. Paula managed to keep her mouth shut to allow Edna to concentrate. A heavy curtain of gloom covered us, and I had the most dreadful feeling that something awful was just about to happen.

I must have blacked out, because I don't remember the car leaving the road. I recall waking up out of a daze, startled because the car window was over my head, and not to my left where it should have been. I felt a terrible pain in my neck, but was able to move it from side to side, which meant that it was pulled, but not broken.

I undid the seatbelt that held me in place, and although the buckle was crushing my ribs terribly, I was nevertheless grateful for it. I would have flown right through the window without it.

Frantically, instinctively, I tried to force the car door open, first with my arms, and then with both feet. Gravity was against me, and I couldn't get it to budge. It was like attempting to lift a slab of concrete. I started screaming.

"Edna, Edna…I can't get the door open."

"Can you get out the window?" she said. Her voice was weak, muffled.

"Are you hurt?" I cried.

"I'm okay," she said. "I'm all right."

"Try to get out through the window," she repeated.

I grabbed the handle and strained to roll it open, but it was difficult. It must have been frozen, because it took every bit of energy I had to get it to move that first inch.

"Can you get out?" she hollered.

I put my hands on the door and pulled myself up. I was able to lever myself to an upright position, then I wormed my way to freedom.

Once out of the car, I could see exactly what had happened. We'd never made it to the main road. The car had overturned near the small viaduct; not completely, because we weren't driving very fast, but it was lodged sideways in the ditch immediately beside the overflowing creek. The water was circling around us, and I had the most horrible vision of it filling the car slowly but surely, eventually drowning both Edna and Paula.

Edna's window was plastered with ice and she couldn't get the handle to turn. We had to work hard to get the door open. I pulled and she pushed and finally we did it. I gave her my hand, grasped the side of the car for balance, and she dragged herself out. It wasn't until I went to do the same for Paula that I realized she had lost consciousness, probably from the cold. She was dressed for an evening stroll down the streets of Manhattan, not a precarious drive through the backwoods of Waterloo.

And because she was in the passenger side of the vehicle, and that was the side that had slid into the ditch, it would be much harder to get her out. Impossible, even.

"We can't do it," said Edna. "We haven't got the strength to pull her up." She attempted to walk to the other side of the car but faltered. I wondered what was wrong. She reached down and felt her ankle.

"Is it broken?" I asked.

"I don't think so, but I can't put any pressure on it. Not the least little bit." She winced with pain. "We've got to get help." Edna was trembling. "We've got to get her out."

It was nothing short of a disaster, and with all the Mennonite folks up in Floradale, I had nowhere to turn. They would have come at a moment's notice and towed out the car. And they could have attended to Paula as well. I felt totally helpless.

"Are you sure the two of us can't drag her out?" I asked.

"Not without help," she replied.

"I guess you're right," I said.

Edna took a deep breath. "We've got to pull this car out of the ditch. Then we can open the passenger door and get her out that way."

I guess the Joan of Arc in me boiled to the surface because that was the moment I decided that I would be the one to do it. "Without any phone connections, we can't call for help. And all my Mennonite friends are in Floradale," I said. "But the good thing is that my family traveled there with the Webers. Della and the cutter are at home."

"What are you saying, Beth?" Edna's face was fraught with anxiety. She was bright red, not only from panic, but from the penetrating wind. I knew I had to act. If there was one thing I had learned as a Mennonite, it was self-sufficiency.

"I will get Della and the cutter, and she will pull out your car," I told Edna. "Then we'll take Paula home and put her by the fire."

I hadn't forgotten my bad experience with driving the cutter, but I could not surrender to fear. I realized that if I took another spill—if my wrist suffered another injury—it would mean I might never draw again. But there were no other options. We had to get the lawyer out of that vehicle and to a warm place.

I didn't give Edna a chance to argue. My hands trembled like jelly and my teeth chattered like chipmunks, but I ran home faster than I ever had in my life. It felt like it took a year to get there, but in fact, it took only ten minutes. I knew that in order to keep Della on a straight course, I would need a tight hold on the reins, so I dashed into the kitchen to get my father's special driving gloves. Topper must have sensed the state I was in, because he barked hysterically when I threw open the door.

I dragged Grand-mama's step stool to the cupboard so that I could reach the top shelf. I couldn't take time to light a kerosene lamp, so it was just like trying to find matches at Edna's. And since only my left arm would stretch that high, I had to grope around, awkwardly touching various things in an attempt to find the gloves. My father's hat was there. And some kind of large salad bowl. Then I felt the black-covered recipe book.

The recipe book.

I held it in my shuddering hand.

Was it a symbol of my culture, my legacy, or was it my chance to become a professional artist?

Was it a way to buy things for my parents that they otherwise couldn't afford?

Would it mean a new roof?

Everything bounced through my mind at once.

For one brief second, one tiny moment, I thought about sticking that book in my pocket and savagely turning it over to the lawyer. I thought about becoming a great artist. I thought about how my life would change. I thought about how famous I could become.

But then I remembered what my grandmother had said.

Our heritage is not for sale.

I was a Mennonite, and I was grateful for the self-reliance that had been shown to me by my parents and instilled in me since birth. How warm it felt to walk into that kitchen when everything else around me was cold and dark because people were reliant on heat from a source other than the trees that grew around them. I was honored that we depended upon nothing but the sweat of our brow and our faith in God.

I was proud to come from a family that could not be bought, no matter how much they needed money.

The black book dropped to the floor as I reached for the kid gloves and stuffed them into my coat pocket. I jumped down, then kicked the stool away from the door. Without thinking, I quickly picked up the recipe book, slid it into a desk drawer, and dashed to the barn.

I knew how to hitch Della. I had seen it done hundreds of times, and while she'd likely never had it done in such a haphazard way, she was a good sport and didn't move around too much. I tossed a blanket on her back, threw the bridle over her neck, and connected up her harness to the cutter. I took an extra blanket to keep Paula warm. Last of all, I found the thickest tow rope we had—the one we used to haul our maple syrup wagon from the sugar bush—and flung it onto the seat.

I noticed that one of the runners was slightly bent and thought back to when I overturned. I would be in a ditch or river in no time. I had watched my father bang it into place more than once, and that was exactly what I did. I used the big thick-headed mallet, hammering with all my might. I hated taking time to do it, but I remembered my father telling me how, with a cutter, the runners were much straighter than with the sleigh; they had to be, to keep it running smooth. He also told me that turns had to be taken wider and slower than with the large sleigh. I thought about using the sleigh, but it would have been impossible for me to handle if something went wrong.

For a split second I wondered if I should just ride Della. But without the cutter, I would have nothing I could hitch the rope to. And what about Paula and Edna? They'd need to ride in the cutter.

"Come on, girl," I said. "You can do this." I think I was the one who needed convincing. I was the one who needed the pep talk. More than once, I reminded myself that we'd only be driving down a back road. There was very little traffic in the good weather, let alone during a storm. We'd be fine.

Della didn't like the ice at all and stopped short at the end of our lane. I didn't want to use the whip, but I had no choice. I was as gentle as I could be, but I knew that if I was anything less than firm, she would balk. I had never whipped Della before, not ever. It was hard for me to do that. I steered her very gingerly and was careful not to make any sharp turns.

We started down the road at a walking pace, then she moved faster, into a trot. The ice rain hit my face, stinging my skin like cold drops of acid. Della had her blinders on which helped somewhat, but even she was tilting her head on an angle in an attempt to avoid being pelted.

I could see a red glow coming from the taillights of Edna's car, reflecting into the water that swirled around it. Della and I trotted our way to where she was. I couldn't even feel my hands inside those kid gloves. Whether that was due to the cold or my nerves, I did not know, but I kept going. I never looked back.

"You did it! You got the horse!" cried Edna. "And thank God you did. Not even one car has come down this road." She was in terrible pain with her ankle, and as much as I wished I could help her, it was Paula who needed my attention first.

I leaned in through the open window and positioned the blanket over top of the lawyer as best I could. It was thick, woven from wool, and would help maintain some of her body heat.

"Do you have a trailer hitch, Edna?" I asked.

"I do!" she exclaimed. "I had it installed for my trip to Cape Breton."

The hitch had not sunk beneath the water, which

was a godsend because it would have been an impossible task if we couldn't connect the rope to something welded onto the vehicle. If we had to use the bumper or even the undercarriage, it might have snapped and we'd be unable to drag the car out in one piece. Edna's vehicle was small, but even so, if we pulled the bumper off, we wouldn't have much hope of getting it out of the water.

I connected one end of the towrope to the trailer hitch, and the other end to the strong metal brace of our cutter. It was at least fifty years old, maybe more, but as solid as the rock of Gibraltar. I picked up the whip, gritted my teeth, and mustered every bit of strength I had within me.

"Come on, Della," I hollered. "It's up to you now! You've got to do this for us!"

She balked several times. Our horse was used to working on all sorts of jobs, but was not accustomed to automobiles and it took her a few minutes to agree to what I was asking her to do. But agree she did and because of her might, and my determination, we pulled until we got that car from the ditch. It drew us back more than once when Della lost her grip on the ice, but we did not yield. We did not relent. We got it out of the water, and up to the road.

Edna was in tears.

"Good God, Beth," she said. "What would I have done without you? What would I have done?"

It must have been the movement of the car that woke Paula. She began to mumble incoherently. There was a huge dent in the passenger side of Edna's car, but I managed to yank the door open.

"Are you okay?" I said softly. Paula did not answer me.

"I don't think she can stand up," said Edna.

"The blanket must be keeping her body temperature from falling too far," I said. "She isn't shivering like she was before."

Edna was alarmed by my remark. "That may be a sign that her condition is getting worse," she said. "The body slows down if the temperature drops too far."

It was clear that Paula required urgent medical help.

"Can you help me to get her into the cutter?"

"I don't know," said Edna. "I can't put any pressure on my ankle whatsoever."

There was no way that I could lift Paula up by myself.

And even if I could, taking her back to my house was not going to be enough. She needed to get to a hospital.

At that point, it dawned on me that I would have to drive Della out to the highway to get help, and that would mean sharing the road with traffic. To this day, I don't know how I found the nerve to do it. The only way I can explain it is that everything was so bleak, I figured it couldn't get any worse. I took the reins, gave poor Della another wallop on the hips, and headed to the highway. In a way, the ice was a blessing for us, because it kept the cutter moving.

Because of the storm, the traffic was not as heavy as it usually was, but everyone seemed to be in a mad rush nevertheless. Cars and trucks were swishing past Della and me, angrily honking at us because they didn't want to share the road. They resented having to slow down and wait for a moment to get around us. I tried several times to get a passing motorist to stop, waving and shouting, but not one did. Not even one.

I drove on towards Elmira, figuring I would eventually be able to flag down a police officer. I had only traveled a mile or two when fate finally took a turn for the better. I spotted a cruiser parked on the shoulder; a young constable was directing traffic through an intersection that was without lights. He called for an ambulance, and my work was done.

Like coming to the surface after a deep, deep dive,

my spirits soared as I circled back to the side road and took Della home. I can't even remember reaching our laneway, I must have floated there on a cloud of elation. I knew that my family was back because I saw smoke billowing from all of the chimneys. And someone had been to the barn, because there was a lantern left lit, hanging near the door.

I took time to give Della some fresh alfalfa to eat and made sure her bedding was clean. I dried her off, then hung the harness, bridle, and blanket in their proper places on the wall.

"You were a good girl, Della," I told her. "The best horse in the world."

She looked tired, and no wonder, so I left her to rest and carried the lantern to the house. I could hardly wait to tell my parents and Grand-mama what I had done. And wouldn't my sister and brother love to hear about it? I was nearly skipping my way through the ice rain.

I opened the back door and saw my parents and grandmother seated at the kitchen table. My brother stood up, gave me an odd look, and walked into the other room. Sarah was nowhere around, which told me she had likely been sent to bed. I knew immediately that something was wrong.

I can't recall any other time in my life when Grand-mama was so enraged that she was—at least temporarily—rendered speechless.

Topper was the only one who greeted me. He bounded over the moment I came through the door. I gave him a hug, but it wasn't much of one. I felt like I had just walked into an inquisition.

"What's wrong?" I asked.

My mother began to cry.

"How could you do it to us, Beth?" said my father. "How could you? I thought we raised you better."

"What?" I was totally mystified. "Are you angry that I took the cutter? You won't be when I—"

Grand-mama flew into a rage.

"You have defied us, and you have disparaged your whole community."

"But—"

"You are a disgrace to us all, and I want nothing to do with you."

My voice throbbed with sadness. "How can you say that?"

"You know that you are not allowed to drive the cutter," said my mother, "but you did it, just to take that woman lawyer for a ride." She wiped tears from her eyes. "You were so eager to please her, you risked driving Della in this kind of weather! But even worse than that—"

My grandmother stomped across the kitchen floor, stood on the step stool, then reached up to the top of the oak cupboard. "You gave her the family recipe book."

I couldn't speak.

"Well, didn't you?" She pointed at me in such a way that I felt her finger go clear through my forehead. "I wondered where you had gone with the cutter, but it didn't take long to figure it out. I knew there had to be a reason why you were so anxious to go to Edna's cottage today." She pointed again. "You are a wicked girl. You sold us out."

I don't know how long Edna and the officer had been standing there. They had sent Paula to the hospital before coming to see if I had made it back safely. My brother had taken them in through the front door when all the hollering was going on. Edna hobbled towards my grandmother, using the officer's shoulder like a crutch. I raced past them and ran to my room. I was completely and utterly devastated.

"Clara!" I heard Edna exclaim as I flew up the stairs. "You don't know what you're saying!"

CHAPTER TEN

"So Miss Logan made it back to New York safely, did she?" asked Grand-mama, pouring big mugs of steaming coffee for Edna, my mother, and herself. She carried a small jug of thick yellow cream to the table. Sarah and I had glasses of milk, and there was a tray of squares and cookies in front of us. The sun was beaming through our window, the baby was banging on her highchair, and I thought to myself that spring would soon be making its arrival. It had been two weeks since the night of the ice storm, and the weather had taken a major turn for the better.

"She did make it home," said Edna. "And she wants me to let you know that she'll be coming back this summer. She wants to see the covered bridge." Edna laughed. "She told me that if she could spend a little more time with you, her ulcer would be cured once and for all."

After Grand-mama had misjudged me so harshly, she discovered a well of forgiveness within herself, even for lawyers from New York City. I think that she was actually looking forward to seeing Paula again. After what happened that night in the ice storm, she allowed her to borrow the family recipe book, just as long as it was returned in one piece and none of our people had to testify in court. Paula did not win her case but benefited from her time with us in other ways. She returned to Waterloo often, and always stopped by to visit. She wasn't so pressured; she was content with life. And I never saw her take another antacid.

"I am glad Paula wasn't seriously injured," said Mama, and I nodded in agreement.

"How is your ankle?" I asked Edna.

"Oh, it's fine. I limped around for a while, but I'm coming along." She smiled. "I hope I never have to live through something like that again." She looked directly at Mama. "I only wish you could have seen your daughter in action. It was a sight to behold."

We Mennonites are not allowed to be prideful, but we are human, and can't do much about physiological reactions. The blood rushed to my face, and I must have looked a sight because my mother pushed back my bangs, felt my forehead, and then rubbed my arm. "She's a wonderful girl."

Edna looked at her watch. "We'd better get going, Beth," she said. "Mrs. Gladstone will be waiting for us. You don't want to be late for your first class." She smiled. "Not when you are going to be her best student."

"I packed up the eggs and butter," said Grand-mama, "and a dozen cookies, too."

That was more than Mrs. Gladstone had asked for, and I appreciated the gesture.

"Gumdrop cookies!" said Sarah. She had finally convinced our grandmother to bake the cookies she wanted. She picked up two at once, then started pulling the colored jellies out, eating them first.

"Here," said Mama, passing the plate to Edna. "Have one for the road."

Edna took a bite. Then another. Then she broke out laughing.

"What's wrong?" said Grand-mama.

"You won't believe this." She could barely get out the words for laughing so hard. "The cookie part is crispy…and the gumdrops are chewy!" We all joined in the laughter, even my grandmother. It was a moment I will never forget. Edna put down her mug and added, "But let's keep it to ourselves, shall we?"

Because I'd spent so much of my spare time sketching, it didn't take long for me to learn to work with color. I used the little set of paints that Edna gave me for months, until they were almost gone. I painted our fieldstone house, the sugar bush, Topper, our dairy cows—even the chickens. Sometimes I did landscapes of the meadow, and the wildflowers that grew there.

Mrs. Gladstone was a good teacher, and she was happy with how quickly I progressed. She provided me with better quality paper, and larger sheets, so that I didn't have to limit my subject matter. After six months of lessons, she encouraged me to enter one of my paintings into the county fair competition. First prize was a set of Winsor and Newton watercolors— the full range of hues—something I had only dreamed of owning. I couldn't afford to have my painting framed by a professional, but my father made me a lovely one from wood he cut himself.

My whole family came to the fair. Even Grandmama. She said that she wanted to take a look at the quilts, but I knew better. She wouldn't say so, but she was proud that my painting had been accepted into the competition. The only one that wasn't nervous was Rebecca. She just chortled and kicked her feet the whole time. The rest of us watched intensely as three judges walked up and down past the rows and rows of paintings on display in the fine-art tent. Edna stood with my family as we awaited the final decision.

You could have heard a pin drop when the judges gathered at the front of the tent, scrutinized the entries one last time, and then announced their choice.

"Our decision was unanimous," said one of the judges. "First place goes to Miss Beth Betzner, for her glorious painting, *Daybreak*."

When he pinned the blue ribbon on my picture, Mama cried.

It was a scene from her garden, her peach-colored roses against a blue sky, and it still hangs in the parlor to this day.

END NOTE

In a *Globe and Mail* article from 1985, June Callwood called it "The Great Cookie War." For cookbook author Edna Staebler and her Old Order Mennonite friends in Waterloo, the whole thing was foolishness! The recipe for rigglevake cookies had, after all, been scribbled in Bevvy Martin's little black book for decades. Why all the fuss now? When it was published in Edna's bestselling and world-famous *Food That Really Schmecks*, no one could have known the brouhaha that one recipe could create. But it did.

The situation began eleven years after *Schmecks* had been published. Procter and Gamble (P&G) had put eighteen million dollars into bringing a new cookie to market, one that would be crispy on the outside but chewy in the middle. They patented their secret recipe in 1979. When rival Nabisco began baking similar cookies, P&G sued for infringement of copyright. And both sides were desperate to get their hands on that little black recipe book. Why? Because it was from that book that Edna Staebler copied the recipe for rigglevake cookies, and rigglevake cookies are crispy and chewy at the same time. And since the recipe was published in *Schmecks*, Nabisco argued that P&G had no case.

Through it all, Edna Staebler fiercely protected her Mennonite friends and eschewed offers from radio and television stations—she even declined the chance to appear on the Jay Leno show.

Caroline Stellings kept up a personal correspondence with the cookbook author, and was so impressed by her charismatic personality, that she always knew that one day she would write a book about Edna Staebler and her involvement in "The Great Cookie War."

Acknowledgments

The author wishes to thank Gillian Rodgerson for her invaluable help with the manuscript, Jordan Ryder for her additions, and the wonderful women at Second Story Press who are always such a joy to work with. The author would also like to thank the Ontario Arts Council for providing two grants for the writing of this novel.

About the Author

Caroline Stellings is an award-winning author and illustrator. She is the author of the Nicki Haddon Mystery series, and her book *The Contest*, part of the Gutsy Girl series, won the 2009 ForeWord Book of the Year Award and was a finalist for the 2010/11 Hackmatack prize. Her novel *Freedom's Just Another Word* was a finalist for the 2017 Geoffrey Bilson award. Besides her many books for children and young adults, she is also the writer of *The Nancy Drew Crookbook*, a long-running series in *The Sleuth* magazine. She lives in Waterdown, Ontario.